CARD, KILL THEM ALL

CARD, KILL THEM ALL

A CARD JORDAN WESTERN
BOOK 1

MONTY R. GARNER

WOLFPACK
PUBLISHING
— EST 2013 —

IN MEMORY OF

Woods Garner
Lera Garner
Franklin Garner
Sue Janoe
Billye Gallagher
Charlie Toliver
Juanita Toliver
Charles Toliver

I LOVE YOU ALL.

CARD, KILL THEM ALL

CHAPTER ONE

S ixteen-year-old Card Jordan was returning home from his first solo hunting trip by himself. He was proud of his camping and hunting skills since he'd shot and skinned three deer on the first day out.

It was almost noon of the third day since he'd left his family to go on this adventure, and he was almost back to the ranch. The weather was exceptionally nice for October 28, 1875.

He was no more than a mile from home when he came across the hoof prints of five shod horses. His horse, Smoke, came to a stop as Card pulled back on the bridle reins. While looking toward the direction they were traveling, a sick, upset feeling formed in the pit of his stomach. *Could this be the five men I saw on the trail the day I left to go hunting?* he thought to himself.

Based on the direction of the tracks, they were headed straight toward his home, and he was concerned for his family's safety. If it was the same five men he'd seen, there was no telling what they might do to his family.

Recollection of what the leader looked like came back to him. The man was dressed in black clothing and wore a fancy pearl-handled gun like an outlaw or gunfighter would wear. All the black clothing had left Card with an ominous feeling, and the scowl on the man's face was tight and resentful. If he had been the boss, then the rest of the men had to be just as capable of committing crimes, or they wouldn't have been riding with him. Young Card made the assumption they were the type of treacherous men his pa had warned him to stay clear of, based on what he remembered when he saw them on the trail.

Reaching down, he felt the grips on his gun and remembered he hadn't put the bullets back in it since he'd practiced his fast draw earlier. They were still in his coat pocket. Nervousness overcame him as he pulled the gun out of its holster and started to reload the chambers. His hand was shaking so badly that he dropped a bullet. When his gun was loaded, he slid it back in the holster and made himself a mental note to never forget to reload his gun again.

Touching his heels against the sides of his horse, he continued on home cautiously. As he approached the ranch house, he rode into the trees that grew in the creek bottom close by. He pulled his horse and the two pack horses to a halt and took notice that something seemed very wrong.

"Oh Lord, help us."

There wasn't any movement, no noise of any kind, and no smoke coming from the chimney. There was always smoke coming out of the chimney because Mama was always cooking food this time of day. His siblings or his pa should be outside doing chores.

That sick, upset feeling was back again as he realized things were not normal and that he needed to be careful as he approached the house.

Instincts told him to charge in and see what was happening, but he knew better. Those men could be in the house holding his family and waiting for him to come home. He'd have to sneak up to the house and investigate further before making any kind of aggressive action.

He dismounted at the creek bottom, tied the horses to some saplings, and unpacked the double-barrel shotgun. While easing through the trees toward the house, he paused every few feet to look for any sign of trouble or movement. Stopping at the edge of the trees, he had a good view of the north side of the house and the backyard.

There was something on the ground outside the back door that wasn't normally there. It looked like a pair of boots. He wondered why boots would be out there.

Carefully he moved to a new position and saw something else. He couldn't figure out exactly what it was...but it looked like a body.

Now he was frightened. Was it one of his family members?

His heart was pounding through his chest, and he could hardly stay focused to figure out what to do next.

He waited, staying very still, listening and

watching the house. He was sweating and terrified but knew it was time to make a move and look inside the rooms.

He ran in a low crouch as fast as he could until he reached the north kitchen wall.

While standing still he took in deep breaths of air and placed his ear to the wood, listening for any sound from inside. When he didn't hear anything, he eased along the wall to the kitchen window.

He stood up slowly, looked in the window and saw five dirty place settings and a bunch of dirty bowls still on the table. Mama would never leave the table looking like that. Something was certainly wrong.

Card was so scared now that his shirt was becoming drenched from sweat and his hands were shaking.

He had to see what was on the ground by the back door, so he eased to the corner and looked around it. What he saw was a gruesome sight and he fell to his knees, weeping in agony.

As his emotions took over, Card could barely see for the tears streaming from his eyes, but he could manage to see Pa, his sisters, and his brother all lying in the grass covered with blood.

They were so still, and the color had left their faces. He knew they were all dead.

But where was Mama?

Totally heartbroken and devastated, Card sat weeping. He wanted to go to them and hold each one in his arms. He couldn't think straight; all he could do was sob and stare at their lifeless bodies.

Pa had served twenty years in the Army fighting

Indians and outlaws and now this had happened to him at his own home.

He shook his head, unable to comprehend how anyone could kill his innocent brother and sisters in cold blood. They had never hurt one person in their short lives. He looked up at the sky, hurt and confused.

God, why? Lord why?

I've got to get in the house and find Mama.

Turning his face away from his dead family, he started to quiet his breathing and get control of himself.

His thoughts began to turn from sorrow and despair to anger. This was wrong in every way imaginable. Card wanted to get mad and cause pain to the men that did this.

It was time to get up and continue investigating and find Mama. She could be hiding or lying injured somewhere.

After he stood up and collected his thoughts, he wiped the tears from his eyes with his shirt sleeve and leaned the shotgun against the wall by the back door. With his pistol in his hand, he went hurriedly inside the house.

There were two separate bloodstains on the kitchen floor where his sisters had probably been shot. A picture of them standing at the sink washing and drying the dishes, giggling and getting each other wet, came to his mind.

He began to search through the rest of the house, first by going down the hallway to the bedrooms. He could tell by the blood on the floor and wall that someone had been shot coming out one of the bedrooms. That had to have been his brother Ben, or maybe Pa.

It was evident the men had searched the bedrooms. Drawers were pulled out, the contents scattered on the floor, and some of the furniture was overturned.

It looked like they had stayed the night and slept in the house; all the beds were messed up and nasty.

The more he saw, the angrier he became. "They murdered my family and then had the nerve to sleep in our beds," he said through clenched teeth.

But where was Mama?

Card went to the living room and saw Pa's overturned chair stained with blood and a bigger stain on the floor. He knew this had to have been where they killed Pa. The stains in the hallway had to have been from Ben.

The front door was slightly open, so he walked over and examined it for damage, The lock and doorframe were shattered from someone kicking it in. He saw a muddy boot mark on the door. He went to the back door and inspected it also and saw that the lock had been shattered.

He tried to piece together what had happened.

Some of the men must have come through the front door and killed Pa, and probably at the same time some more men had come through the back door and killed the girls while they were washing dishes. He assumed Ben had come out of his bedroom to investigate and one of the murderers shot him.

It had probably happened so quickly that they never even knew what was happening.

Card went to the front window and looked out at the yard, barn, and corral. It was then that he noticed something on the ground by the barn. It looked like a body.

Closing his eyes, he silently prayed that it wasn't Mama.

That sick feeling came back over him, though, and he shook with fear and anger.

He stood there thinking, *I need to go look in the barn but, there is too much open space between it and the house to cross the yard directly.* He decided to go out the back door and circle around behind the barn.

As Card approached the barn from the rear, he saw Mama lying on the ground, dead. His first instinct was to check to make sure she was dead, but he could tell that she was. Placing his hands over his face, he closed his eyes for a moment to try to clear his mind.

What do I do? I need to think. I must keep moving.

He remembered then that the front barn doors were partially open. He eased by Mama, trying not to look at her as he proceeded down the side of the barn toward the front corner. He paused to listen for any sounds before moving to the front of the structure where the doors were. As he slowly advanced toward the open doors, he stopped to calm his nerves and that was when he noticed several horses were missing from the corral.

Pa's sorrel stud and two broodmares were gone, and he knew then that the murdering thieves had already left.

They'd killed his family, eaten his food, slept in his family's beds, and even stolen their horses.

Card walked away from the barn feeling like his whole world was now destroyed. He went to his mama's side and started sobbing as he stood looking down at her. But something caught his attention through his salty tears. It was crudely written in the soil. He wiped his eyes and blew his nose as he moved closer.

Inscribed in the dirt by her bloody fingers were four words. CARD KILL THEM ALL.

The tears and weeping began again as he fell to the ground, taking hold of his dead mama and placing her head in his lap. Trembling fingers moved her hair ever so gently out of her face and he looked at her, thinking. *How could anyone do such a thing to her?*

He sat holding his mama in his arms for a long time. Finally, he looked again at what she had written in the dirt and composed himself.

"Mama, I promise you, Pa, Mattie, Ben, and Shelia that I will hunt down every one of those murdering polecats and make them pay."

This was a promise he had to keep, and he knew what had to be done. KILL THEM ALL!

He pulled his old, battered hat off his head and laid it on the ground so he could set his mama's head on it.

Getting to his feet, he began looking around the yard. There were bloodstains on the ground about thirty feet away, so he walked in that direction and looked around more, trying to figure out what had happened.

His father had taught him to have an eye for details while learning to track animals, so looking for clues was second nature for Card.

It seemed Mama had been going toward the house when she was shot, because the front of her dress was covered in blood and dirt. From the marks on the ground, she must have crawled or dragged herself to the spot where he found her.

"Poor Mama," Card said. "What agony you must've gone through knowing everyone had been killed. You knew you were dying when you wrote this message to me, didn't you?"

He bent down to pick her up in his arms and carried the limp body into the house. He took the corpse to the bedroom and placed it on the bed and covered her up with a blanket, still crying.

While composing himself, he went back outside and began bringing each family member in the house, placing them on their beds and covering them up. It was the hardest thing he had ever done, having to carry his baby brother and sisters in the house that way. He sat on the bed with each one and cried for the loss of their lives.

It took all his might to get his pa in the house, but through his anger and sorrow he managed to find the strength and power to get him onto the bed with Mama.

When he finished bringing in all the bodies, he went once more out the back door. There were his pa's boots. He picked them up and set them inside the kitchen door.

Card noticed he had blood on his clothes now. That was the moment he knew that he was going to get revenge on the murderers that killed his family, no matter what. He was so angry that he pulled his gun out and started firing into the sky. His finger kept pulling the trigger even after all the bullets were gone and he was listening to the hammer fall on an empty cylinder. Finally getting control of his emotions, he took some deep breaths and opened the cylinder on his gun and reloaded, sliding it back into the holster.

In a semi-daze he went back to his horses and untied them, mounted Smoke, and headed to the neighbor's ranch about two miles away. He would need help burying his family, and to find someone to take care of the ranch when he left to kill the five men.

He was still in a stupor but rode the horses hard, not wanting to waste any time.

The men that had killed his family had no morals or consciences at all. Not only had they murdered five people, but they had also dragged the bodies outside for the varmints and worms to feed on. Hatred built inside the young man's mind and soul. He had a promise to keep, and he needed to get started as quickly as possible.

CHAPTER TWO

Ned knew they were leaving a lot of tracks as they left the ranch, but he intended to try his best to cover their trail.

He was angry and in a foul mood. His men hadn't found anything valuable in the house the previous day, after they'd gone to the trouble of killing everyone. He had been sure there would be something else at the ranch worth stealing besides three horses.

Riding with him was Smokey Thomas, Bill Hill, TC Stewart, and Big Bob Kennon. They were a mean, nasty, vulgar, murderous group of men, and he'd handpicked every one of them to be his associates in crime.

As soon as they got to the creek, he gave his men direction. "Ride in the water and stay in single file until we find a good place to exit," he snapped. "Smokey, make damn sure you don't throw any of your cigarette butts down."

"I ain't gonna throw none down," replied Smokey.

If you wouldn't have one in your nasty mouth all the time, I wouldn't have to keep reminding you, Ned thought.

"We'll ride south until we get close to the Sulphur River then we'll turn northwest," he informed the group.

Ned and his men found a rocky point that protruded into the creek a little way.

Ned turned his horse so he could face his men. "Stay on these rocks as far as we can; if anyone is tracking us it'll be difficult for them to see where we're heading."

"Right," said Bill Hill.

Ned sighed. His men were imbeciles, he was starting to realize. He had to tell them every move to make and had to constantly remind them of what to do when they were on the run.

When they'd ridden hard for about six miles, Ned raised his hand and stopped the group. "We'll rest here a few minutes to give the horses a breather then we'll continue in this direction, since it won't be long until we come to the Sulphur River. We'll turn upstream and ride until dusk. We can then make camp there for the night."

"So, you mean we've got to spend another night in the cold, sleeping on the hard ground?" asked TC. "And we gotta eat Bill's cooking again?"

Ned looked at TC and squinted. "That's right, you will!" he exploded. "Unless we see another house that we could take over like we did last night."

TC looked around at the others and shook his

finger. "Next time, don't anyone shoot the women folks straight away. It's high time we have a little fun first. That oldest girl and the woman could have entertained us all night if we hadn't rushed the house with guns blazing." They all nodded their heads in agreement, even Ned.

TC is right, this time, thought Ned. *We could've had some fun if we'd investigated better. And we probably could have made them tell us where the valuables were hidden. Oh well, that's water under the bridge now.*

"The next time, let me go check the house out first. That way I can call dibs on the pretty ones," exclaimed Bill, while slapping his leg and laughing.

"Look on the bright side of killing all them folks," said Big Bob. "We got to eat good and sleep in nice soft beds, plus when we left there, we took some good food for the trail."

Smokey rubbed out his cigarette. "Leave it to Big Bob to think about food." Everyone laughed.

Ned slapped his horse with the reins. "Let's go, time's a wasting."

They spurred their horses forward and continued toward the river, arriving at midafternoon—much earlier than Ned had expected.

He searched for a place where they could conceal their tracks before turning northwest. He found where the ground was hard since it was mostly clay, and the hard ground would help conceal the tracks.

That night they made camp in a wide gulley where their fire wouldn't be as noticeable to anyone traveling on the well-worn trail. Bill cooked supper and they ate all the food they had. Then they grumbled because there wasn't more. They sat around the campfire and complained about not having any whiskey.

"I still can't believe we didn't find any money in that house," said Ned. "I'll bet they had a hiding place somewhere, and that's where all the valuables were."

He was still frustrated that they had come up empty-handed. *They probably ain't smart enough to find anything hidden,* he reckoned. *I should've searched the house myself.*

"I thought we were going to hit a bank and make a big pile of money," Big Bob commented.

"Yeah, well, I have big plans," said Ned. "I think those plans will pay out nicely and we can live high on the hog for a while."

Everyone was getting a little agitated from being on the run for over four weeks. Their tempers were getting short. Ned knew that a big bank payday would make everyone feel a little better—at least for a little while.

TC said, "I want a soft bed, more food and whiskey, and a woman to snuggle up to. That sounds better than robbing and killing women and kids."

"Don't worry, there will be plenty of that in Paris, Texas," said Ned. "There's a small town called Reno about six miles east of Paris, and that's where we'll make camp tomorrow night," he continued. "I'll find us a spot a little ways outside of town and everyone can rest up while I go and case the place out. I'm pretty sure there's a bank there that'll be easy pickings and provide us spending money for our time in Paris."

They all agreed this was a good plan.

When everyone was in their bedrolls, Ned said, "In a couple of days we'll be living like kings in a nice warm place that is flowing with whiskey, women, and food. Just be patient."

CHAPTER THREE

Card rode into his neighbor's yard and called out when he saw young James Wallace.

"Go fetch your pa. I need your help. Something terrible has happened."

Homer Wallace owned the Lazy H Ranch, along with his wife Helen and three sons, James, Johnny, and Ricky. Homer was a good man and had been on his ranch for thirty years. He was always willing to help his neighbors out in times of need.

The horses were lathered up and winded from the hard ride. Card was dismounting when Homer and the other boys came to greet him.

"What's with all the blood?" asked Homer, as he looked at Card's clothes.

Card said nothing. He walked up to his neighbor with tears streaming down his face.

Homer grabbed Smoke's bridle and told his boys to take the horses and walk them around the yard to cool them off, then give them some water.

Homer took Card by the arm. "Come on inside the house and have a seat," he said.

They walked into the house. "Helen," called Homer toward the kitchen. "Bring Card a glass of water."

The big man put his hand on Card's shoulder. "Card, sit down and tell me what's wrong."

Card was crying as Helen came in with a glass of water and set it on the coffee table. She sat down and put her arm around him, trying to comfort him. When he could talk, Card said, "My family is all dead. They were murdered by five men passing through."

He told them the story about going hunting, seeing the five men on the trail, and about his devastating ordeal of finding his family murdered when he arrived home that very morning.

"I am overwhelmed and heartbroken," Helen told Card. "You and your family have been our friends and neighbors for years. What can we do to help?"

"Will you all come back to the house with me? I want to get the bodies cleaned up before burying them and it wouldn't be right or proper for me to see my mama and sister's nakedness."

"Of course we will," said Helen in a soft voice. "Homer, you tell the boys to harness the horses and hook up the wagon while we gather up some things to take with us."

"Me and the boys can dig the graves while you get everyone cleaned up and ready in the house for burial," said Card. "And I've got deer meat on the packhorses. I'd like for you to take it and put it in your smokehouse so you all can eat it, since I don't need it anymore." Then he broke down crying again.

Homer went outside and gathered the boys. He explained what happened and what he wanted them to do.

He told James, "You ride to the county seat over at Clarksville and notify Sheriff Taylor of what happened. Be sure to take your guns and don't stop until you get there. You may need to spend the night, so take some money for a room. You other boys harness up the horses to the wagon. Rickey, you grab shovels, picks, hammer, and nails, and some boards for grave markers. Johnny, you take all that meat off the pack horses and hang it in the smokehouse. When you boys finish, saddle your horses and move Card's saddle to a fresh horse. Be aware we could be riding into trouble, so take your guns."

When the wagon was loaded and everyone was ready to travel, they headed off toward the Jordan ranch.

Card and the boys rode fast and went on ahead, just in case the murderers were still around. They arrived at the house and Johnny loosened the saddle girths, let the horses drink, and turned them into the corral while Card showed Ricky where their digging tools were.

As the brothers got to work gathering up tools, Card walked around the yard looking at the ground for horse tracks that might show the direction the murderers went when they left. He wanted to find that out before the ground got disturbed by everyone being there. He found tracks that looked like they had ridden toward the creek. It was easy to see eight sets of tracks.

Through all his sadness, he tried to make a plan for the future. Could he do what Mama had told him to do? Could he go from a boy to a man in the span of a day?

Could he actually take another man's life?

Next, he looked for a good shady place to dig graves for his family and decided on the side of the house that got shade from a large red oak tree.

"This is where I want to start digging," he said to the Wallace boys. "I want one big grave where we can lay them all side-by-side in the ground. That way they're all still together."

Card began to walk away but stopped to turn back toward the brothers. "There's something I need to look at, I'll be back in a little while."

It was a slow walk to the creek as he followed the tracks the men had left. He saw where they had entered the water. He went down the stream bank about a quarter of a mile before crossing to the other side and starting back up toward the house. The men tried to conceal their tracks by riding in the water, but that many horses were almost impossible to hide, especially from someone with his tracking skills. His pa had been teaching him to track animals since he was eight years old.

He smiled. *You're not that smart*, he thought. *I'll find your trail and kill every last one of you.* Those words frightened him because he had never thought about taking someone's life until that day, and knew it'd take a great amount of courage to go through with it.

The search would have to wait, and he left the creek bottom and went directly where the Wallace boys were digging the grave.

"Give me the shovel and I'll dig awhile since we only found two shovels in the barn," said Card. "We can take turns until the wagon gets here with the rest of the tools."

In a few minutes, they heard the trace chains rattling on the wagon. "Let's get a drink of water and grab the rest of the supplies off the wagon," Card said.

They went out to meet Homer and Helen and get a drink.

"The door is unlocked, and you can use whatever you need," Card said to Homer and Helen as they dismounted and went into the house.

A few minutes later Card heard Helen calling his name, and turned to find her leaning out the open kitchen window, beckoning him to come in.

Card stepped through the back door, where Homer was getting the hot water and rags ready for Helen.

"Card," said Helen. "I think it's best to just clean the blood off their faces and wrap the bodies in blankets. That way you can say your last goodbyes and we can cover the faces and place each one in the grave."

Homer said, "I'll find Abe's Bible and prepare some words to say for their burial. Then I can start cleaning the blood off the floor."

"That'll be fine," Card replied. "Thank you all so much for helping me. I couldn't have done this without your help, and I appreciate all you are doing."

Helen nodded her head and took the water and

rags back to the bedrooms where she started to work on the bodies.

Card helped Homer find Abe's Bible; it was on the floor by his blood-covered chair. Homer carried it to the kitchen where he and Card cleaned the blood spots off the cover.

Card went back outside where the boys were still digging the grave. After about thirty minutes they were finishing up and removing the remaining loose dirt from the hole.

"Go to the wagon and start cutting boards and making crosses for the grave markers," Johnny told Rickey. "And as soon as you get the boards cut, wait for help before carving their names on the wood."

Card looked the grave over. "Johnny, you go ahead and help Ricky. We've dug the grave deep enough."

Card wanted to go back to the house and check on how things were going with Helen.

He came through the back door to find Homer on his knees, cleaning the blood off the floor. He continued to the bedroom to check on Helen. She was still cleaning the blood off little Shelia.

She looked up and said, "Card, you can go in the other bedrooms and say your goodbyes while I finish up in here."

He nodded and went to his mama and pa's room first. He stood looking at them, tears rolling down his cheeks. He uncovered his pa and felt in the man's pockets for his folding knife and pocket watch. He found the knife, but no watch. The killers must have taken it.

"Pa," Card said angrily. "I'll get your watch back."

He leaned over and kissed his pa's cheek and covered the body back up.

He moved to the other side of the bed and kissed his mama's cheek. He told them he loved them both and would see them again in heaven, but first he was going to send five murdering thieves to hell.

He left their room and went to Mattie's room to say his goodbyes and kiss her cheek. He told her he loved her.

Then to Ben's room. He kissed his brother on the forehead and told him he loved him.

He went to Shelia's room last. Helen was just finishing up, so she stepped out to give him some privacy. His baby sister, only eight years old. He took hold of her hand and cried. Card said goodbye and made his way back into the living room.

Homer walked to the front door and hollered for the boys to come into the house.

"I'll bring the wagon to the front door," he told his boys. "We'll start carrying the bodies out and load them. We can make two trips to get them to the gravesite. I want you to be really careful and show the utmost respect."

When all the bodies were lying beside the large hole. Card, Johnny, and Ricky placed each body in the grave. When Card's family were lying side-by-side in their final resting place, Card and the Wallace family removed their hats. Homer opened the Bible and read Psalm 23 and said a prayer.

Card picked up a shovel and began filling in the hole. Tears were rolling down his cheeks once again.

Homer stopped him and told the boys to finish and place the markers at the head of every person.

CHAPTER FOUR

"Card, let's go to the house. I want to talk to you," said Homer when they had set the last grave marker.

Card followed Homer into the house, and they sat down on the couch.

"What are your plans now that you're all alone here?" asked Homer.

After a few seconds of silence, Card looked up with reddened eyes and said, "Mr. Wallace, follow me back outside."

They walked toward the barn where his mama had been shot. Card pointed to the ground at the note she had written in the dirt.

"She wrote this before she died, and this is my plan."

Homer read the message and nodded his head thoughtfully.

"I made a promise to my family that I'd do what my dying mama asked, and I intend to do just that. I realize it'll be hard and painful to kill those men, but it's something I have to do. I hope you and your family will understand that I must avenge their deaths," said Card as he looked at the ground.

Homer said nothing.

"I'd like for you to take over the ranch for me while I'm gone," Card continued. "You can move all the chickens, horses, hogs, and cattle to your ranch if you need to. I'd ask that someone look in on the house every now and then so no squatters move in. You can sell whatever livestock you see fit to pay for your trouble. We have around three hundred twenty head of cattle. I don't know when I'll be back. I don't know if I'll ever be back. If something happens to me, the ranch is yours."

Homer looked Card in his eyes. "Son, are you sure about this? Maybe you should let the law hunt down those men."

Card glanced at the bloodstains his mama's body had left on the ground. "Mr. Wallace, I made a solemn promise, and I intend to keep it and kill those men."

"I'll discuss this with the boys, as they're the ones that'll have to watch your place and take care of your livestock," said Homer as he put his arm around Card's shoulders.

They walked toward the wagon and Card glanced at the graves. "Please ask Mrs. Wallace to plant some flowers on the grave next spring, since Mama always liked flowers."

"I'm sure she'll like doing that, she thought a lot of your mother," replied Homer.

Card's emotions were still in turmoil and anticipation was building as they came to the Wallace's wagon. "I'll be leaving tomorrow to start hunting for those men that did all this," he said. "And I appreciate you and your family so much. I don't know what I would have done without you all here today."

Homer stood and rubbed his chin in thought before calling his wife and boys to come over to the wagon.

"Card has something important to do, and he'll be gone for a while," said Homer. "We're going to take over running his ranch until he gets back. That'll mean extra work for us all, so I want to know if you're willing to do that."

They all nodded in agreement.

Homer looked Card straight in the eye. "Card, I know you have a promise to keep and we'll respect and support that," he said. "I ask that you don't let it ever cloud your mind or your judgment."

"Yes sir," said Card.

"I know you've got things you want to do here before you leave. We'll gather our stuff and head on home. You're more than welcome to come to our house and spend the night."

"I appreciate the invite, but I have too much to do here," said Card. "I'll come over early in the morning to bring your horse back and collect mine."

"That's fine. I'll meet with Sheriff Taylor when he comes and explain everything we know about the murders," said Homer. "You go ahead and get prepared for your journey before the trail grows cold."

"You be sure to come early tomorrow and have breakfast with us before you leave," said Helen.

"I'd like that, Mrs. Wallace," said Card. "I really do appreciate all you did here today."

Homer and Helen climbed up on the wagon seat and the boys mounted their horses and they all rode out.

Card went to his room and gathered up a change of clothes and put them in a bag before going into his pa's bedroom, where he opened the top dresser drawer and found the snuff can with a key inside. He moved the dresser away from the wall and raised up a trapdoor in the floor. Then he took the key and opened the metal box that was hidden in the small space.

Inside the box was Pa's gun, a .44 Colt. He inspected the gun and its holster, then buckled it around his waist.

It felt good.

He drew the gun once to get a feel for its weight. He proceeded to draw it from the holster a few more times for practice and was satisfied with how it fit his hand. He opened the chamber and loaded it with bullets.

He took three boxes of .44 caliber bullets, and two boxes of .30-.30 shells. Tucked away inside an envelope was some paper money, which he removed and counted—$2,700. He folded the money and put it in the pocket of his britches. Then he put the remaining items back into the box and locked it up. When the trapdoor and furniture was back in place, he put the key back in the snuff can and left the room.

He went into the kitchen and saw his pa's boots still sitting by the back door. He sighed heavily, missing his pa almost more than he could stand. Card sat down on the bare wood floor, untied his brogans, and pulled on the boots. They fit nicely, so he decided to keep them.

Then he went to the washbasin and took his pa's straight razor, mirror, and shaving mug and put them in the travel bag along with his clothes.

He would need to take food, so he went to the smokehouse and found two slabs of bacon and a ham. Back in the kitchen, he took cornmeal, flour, salt, and baking powder.

After he'd gathered his supplies, he put a bucket of water on the stove and when it was almost boiling, he poured it in the sink to wash the dirty dishes the murderers had used.

He washed the soiled dishes and thought about his sisters. They had stood where he was standing now, as the murderers had busted through the back door and shot them. He was in anguish and having a hard time coping with his feelings. He dropped a plate, breaking it. The noise and the mess brought him out of his muddled thoughts and back to thinking clearly.

When he finished with the dirty dishes, he continued to gather up what he wanted to take with him.

He searched through the cupboards and found a flour sack to pack his food in. Next, he went into the living room and removed his pa's Winchester 1873 from over the mantel. Upon opening the lever and checking the chamber, he found it fully loaded. Next came a canteen, rain slicker, and his pa's Calvary hat.

Standing in front of the table with all his supplies on it, Card wondered what he'd forgotten. Gloves, handkerchief, and riding chaps. Winter was coming on and he'd need those things to stay warm. He gathered up the additional items and put them with his other gear.

He decided to go out in the yard and take target practice with his new gun. The Colt was lighter than his own gun and the action was smooth. It was important to make the first shot count, so he paid extra attention to hitting his target. There might only be one chance to fire during a gunfight, so he'd better make the first shot count.

After practicing for thirty minutes, shooting over and over again, he got quicker the more he practiced. It started getting dark, so he went back inside and cook himself some supper.

When he finished eating, he heated enough water to wash up his plate and skillet because he was raised to always clean up after himself.

Card looked over his provisions and supplies one more time and decided he could carry all it on Smoke and one pack horse. Only taking one extra horse would allow him to travel faster than using two.

He went into his room and lay on the bed, thinking about what was ahead of him and how he would have to handle it. It was hard to imagine what lay ahead though, and his mind raced with uncertainties.

Sleep didn't come easy that night. Visions of his family lying dead and cold as the hard earth beneath their bodies kept coming to him and he cried, trying to ease the pain.

He saw images of the men that had done this to his

family, and he got madder and madder at them. But he knew he'd take revenge on them and kill them all.

I'm a sixteen-year-old boy and it's not fair that I've got to do this! Now I've got no family left and I'm going to have to kill five men because of what they did.

Dressing before sunrise, he restarted the fire in the kitchen stove to put on water for coffee.

It would take some time to heat up, so he went to the barn and saddled up the horse he had borrowed from Mr. Wallace. He led the horse to the house and tied him to a porch post, then went inside and drank a cup of coffee.

When he finished his coffee, he grabbed his coat, hat, and gloves, went back outside, and mounted up, heading toward the Lazy H Ranch.

He was cold by the time he arrived and was shivering uncontrollably even though he had his coat and gloves on. He tied the horse and started for the door when Homer opened it and said, "Come on in and get warm."

There was a nice fire in the fireplace, and Card stood in front of it, rubbing his hands together.

"Make yourself at home, Helen will have breakfast ready soon," said Homer. "You can go in the kitchen and get a cup of coffee if you want."

About that time, Helen came in and invited him to come eat. She had eggs, bacon, fried taters, and biscuits sitting on the table. After a prayer, they all went after the food.

When they were finished, Card stood up and thanked them for their hospitality and the good breakfast. "I need to collect my horses and get back home, but I only need one pack horse and would like for you to keep the other one here until I get back."

"Sure, just leave it in the corral and we'll tend to it," replied Homer.

Card hugged each member of the family.

The boys went outside with Card to help get the horses ready. Then he mounted, waved, and tipped his hat before riding off. He never looked back because he was afraid, he would break down and cry if he did. He wanted to get back home, load up, and get on the trail. Daylight was wasting and he had a job to do.

CHAPTER FIVE

Ned and his men were up at sunrise, still complaining about having to sleep on the hard cold ground. Bill made coffee and they ate some ham and skillet bread while trying to work the stiffness and kinks out of their sore joints.

Finally, Ned gave the signal and they loaded up their meager supplies and started out on the day's journey. It was windy and cold, and everyone had to bundle up to try to stay warm. Smokey kept complaining about the biting wind. An hour into their ride, Ned finally had enough of his griping. "Smokey, shut your mouth or I'll do it for you myself."

Smokey scowled at Ned but knew better than to talk back. "All right, Ned, I was just blowing off steam."

Ned paid him no mind and kept going.

After another half hour, Ned's thoughts began to wander. He hoped a bank robbery would pay off enough that they could hole up somewhere warm until spring.

The closer they got to Reno, the more farmhouses they started to see scattered all around the country-side. From the looks of the fields, it appeared everyone was raising mostly cotton nowadays.

Ned knew that when the Texas and Pacific Railroad had been built the year before in 1874, it had brought a lot more people to this area because of the good black soil that was ideal for farming.

A few hours later, Ned halted the men about a mile southeast of Reno. Although it was only midafternoon and there was plenty of daylight left, he wanted to stop and make camp.

"Everyone stay put right here until I get back," he said. "I'm going to ride a circle around this site and make sure there's no one close by that can see us."

TC dismounted and tied his horse to a tree limb, sighing loudly.

"I'm getting a little tired of riding all the time and worrying about someone seeing us," said Smokey. "I think if someone sees us, we just kill them and not worry about any of that."

"You heard what Ned said, Smokey," Big Bob said. "Unless you want to square off against him, I suggest you shut your mouth and do what you're told."

Smokey removed the cigarette from his mouth and started to say something when Ned rode back from checking out a campsite.

Ned could tell something was amiss by the look on Smokey's face. He'd probably been complaining again but wasn't man enough to do it in front of the boss.

Smokey gave Big Bob a nasty look but kept his mouth closed.

"I found a small creek running through some trees where we can make camp," said Ned. "Let's go."

They all followed Ned a short distance to their new camp location. There, Bill made a fire and put water on to boil for coffee while the others tied a couple of tarps between some trees to make a windblock.

Big Bob and TC took care of the horses. Ned and Smokey gathered wood for the fire.

"Ned, when you go into town would you stop by the store and buy me some more tobacky?" asked Smokey.

"Yeah," said Ned. "I'll buy you some this time, but you need to make sure you stock up the next time you're at a store."

When the coffee was ready, everyone sat around the fire talking and relaxing until a couple of hours before sunset.

Ned got up, went to his horse, and swung into the saddle. "I'm going into town now and case out the bank," he said. "Bill, have some supper ready when I get back; it'll probably be after dark by the time I'm finished checking out the town."

Bill looked up in time to see Ned leave. "Sure thing, boss," he called out after him.

Ned rode into town from the east on his way to watch the bank before it closed for the day.

He rode down the main street and looked it over carefully to see where the marshal's office was located and how far the bank was from the saloon, hotels, and boarding houses. He didn't want to take the chance of anyone seeing or hearing them breaking into the bank. He was in luck—the bank was located beside a small store selling ladies' hats and sewing supplies on one side, and a narrow street on the other side. Hardly any foot traffic around.

After finding a good place to tie his horse up, he sat and watched the bank for any sign of a guard and tried to determine the amount of business being transacted this time of day.

From his vantage point, he observed the town and especially the bank for about thirty minutes. Not a single customer came or went from the building. Another good sign.

Ned left his horse and walked across the street, opened the door, and went up to the teller window. He handed the man a one-hundred-dollar bill and asked, "Sir, can I get change for this? Preferably four twenties and two tens."

"I've already placed my cash box in the safe," said the teller. "But it won't be no trouble at all to make change for you."

Ned nodded his head and watched the teller walk over and unlock a door that looked like a closet being used as a safe. Ned was surprised that the door was a normal wooden slab door and had only one lock securing it.

Ned smiled as he waited for his change, *this will be easy pickin's and he doesn't have a clue who I am.*

The clerk came back and counted out the bills as he placed them on the counter. "There you go, sir. Is there anything else I can do for you today?"

"No, that's all for today," said Ned. "It's always a pleasure doing business with a good bank."

He picked his money up from the counter and walked out the door, heading down the street about a block to the mercantile store.

He bought two bags of rolling tobacco for Smokey and a sack of hard candy for himself and his men.

The sun was about to set, and Ned was getting hungry. He left the store and walked leisurely back to his horse, mounted up, and rode down the street to the edge of town. Then he crossed over to the other side and rode behind the buildings so he could get a good look at the back door of the bank and the surrounding area.

He rode slow and observed every detail. There was a large unoccupied field with a grove of trees directly behind the bank and no houses within two blocks of the building. He was satisfied that no one would see them when they robbed the bank. He put together a plan for later that night as he rode out of town and back to camp.

Bill had supper cooked, and hot, strong coffee on the fire when Ned got back.

Smokey looked over at Ned and asked, "Did you get me some tobacky?"

Ned didn't say anything but handed him his tobacco and set the sack of hard candy down by his own bedroll.

"I bought y'all a little something sweet for after supper," said Ned. "And I'll go over the plan for tonight after we eat."

When everyone was finished eating and had put

their plates back in their belongings, Ned gathered his men around the fire.

"This is the plan for how we're gonna rob the bank tonight," he said. "We'll bed down early and get up at three. Then we'll ride almost all the way into town. There's a small grove of oak trees behind the bank where we can leave our horses."

Ned looked at Smokey. "Smokey, you'll stay with the horses and keep them quiet. And don't tie them up, I want you to hold the reins in your hands in case we have to leave in a hurry."

Next, he looked at Bill. "You go to the east side of the bank next to the store and stay in the shadows to conceal yourself. Keep an eye on the street for someone that may walk by."

"Right," said Bill.

"Ned, how come the others get in on all the fun and I have to keep the horses?" asked Smokey.

TC spoke up, pointing a finger at Smokey. "Shut up, Smokey. All you do is gripe anymore."

Ned slapped TC on the back. "TC, you stay at the back of the bank and keep an eye out, and if either you or Bill see anyone coming knock on the wall three times. If you can kill whoever it is without making any noise, go ahead and do it, is that clear?"

Bill and TC both smiled, and TC said, "It'll be our pleasure."

Ned went on talking. "Me and Big Bob will smash the lock on the back door and go after the money. I'm familiar with the inside of the bank and know where it is, so's we can go ahead and make ourselves a withdrawal."

Everyone laughed and Bill asked, "Ned, how much money do you think's in the bank?"

"I don't think it's a lot, since it's a small farming town," said Ned. "But you never know. Some of these farmers could have a sizable amount deposited there."

"Yeah, well, it's more than we have now," said Bill.

Smokey rolled a cigarette and stuck it in his mouth. "I'm sorry for complaining, fellers. I'm just ready for some money and a soft bed and a woman."

TC looked at Smokey and smiled. "It's about time you finally apologized for something."

"Hey, y'all can leave old Smoke alone, he's my little buddy," said Big Bob, laughing.

Shortly thereafter, they went to sleep. Three a.m. would come too soon.

Ned was the first to wake up. He rustled everyone out of their bedrolls, which was difficult since it was cold, and everyone was grumpy. They didn't take time to make coffee; they just saddled up their horses and started into town.

Ned led the way to the place they were going to leave the horses. They dismounted and Smokey took hold of their reins while the rest of the gang made their way toward the bank.

Ned and his men walked slowly and carefully, hardly making any noise because they didn't want to alert someone of their presence.

Ned and Big Bob stayed in the shadows at the back door of the bank while the others got in their positions as lookouts.

When it was time to get to work, Ned stuck his hunting knife in between the door and its frame, jimmying the lock open. He gave the door a hard push, and it swung inward, screeching on rusty hinges. They walked into the bank with guns drawn and proceeded down a short hallway to the teller's door.

Big Bob gave it a kick, shattering the lock. The door pivoted open, banging against the wall behind it.

Ned knew the layout of the bank, so he felt along the wall until he found the closet door.

Big Bob kicked it in too, and they went inside, pushing the door closed behind them. Ned lit a match so they could see. He located a coal oil lamp and lit it. All the currency was stacked neatly by denominations on a few narrow shelves. Ned took all the money and put it in a canvas bag he had brought with him. Then he blew out the lamp, opened the door, and they felt along the wall back to the teller's door. They continued down the hall, where Ned opened the back door and looked around before they exited out the back.

Ned motioned for Big Bob to stay still and wait while he went around the corner. He motioned for Bill and TC to join him and Big Bob. Ned and his men eased back to where Smokey was waiting. They led their horses on foot for a short distance before mounting and riding back to camp.

When they got back Ned said, "We'll break camp now and load up our belongings because we're riding to Paris."

They gathered all their things and started off toward Paris, first by riding south and then around Reno so they wouldn't be seen.

A little way out from Paris, Ned brought them to a stop. It was already daylight and people were up and about, beginning their daily chores.

"When we get close to Paris," he said, "we'll ride around to the north of town and come in from the west to throw off anyone that might see us ride in. Go ahead and board your horses at two different livery stables once we get there."

"Who do you want me to ride in with, Ned?" asked Bill.

Ned looked frustrated and let out a sigh. "I don't care, just pick someone, Bill."

Bill threw up his hands because of Ned's remark. "All right, Big Bob and me will come in together."

"Big Bob, you tell the livery stable owner where you stop at, that the sorrel is for sale and maybe both of the pack horses," said Ned. "They're slowing us down and we don't need them anymore."

Big Bob took the pack horses' reins from Smokey and prepared to lead them into town.

Next Ned turned to face his men. "We'll all meet up in a couple of hours at the Longhorn Saloon and get rooms. Don't cause no trouble at the saloon or in town until after we've had some fun and it's time for us to move on."

"Will the saloon be open this early, or do we have to wait outside of town for a while?" asked Bill.

Ned thought for a moment before answering. "Most likely the doors'll be shut, but I know the barkeep and he'll probably be cleaning. I'll make sure he knows you're coming in."

"All right." Bill nodded approvingly.

Ned tipped his hat and took off toward town. He stopped at the first livery stable he came to and boarded his horse, telling the owner that he wanted it fed, watered, and rubbed down.

From the stable, he walked to the Longhorn Saloon. The door was closed but not locked, so he went inside. The owner looked up and saw who it was and said, "Come on in, Ned, long time no see! How have you been?"

"Hello, Harvey, it's been a while. How about pouring me a drink?" Ned sat down on a stool as Harvey poured him a shot of whiskey.

Ned drank it in one gulp and motioned for another. "I've got four men coming into town and we'll need rooms upstairs, if you've got that many vacant."

"I think I can accommodate you and your men, but make sure they stay out of trouble," said Harvey. "I've got a good thing going here, and I don't want the law coming around."

"Of course, they'll stay out of trouble," said Ned. "Now pour me one more drink."

Ned finished that drink too and took a seat at a table where he could watch the street and wait.

About an hour later, he saw Smokey and TC ride into town and drop their horses off at the same livery to get fed, watered, and boarded. Then they came into the Longhorn Saloon. They had a couple of drinks of whiskey at the bar and were told they had rooms upstairs.

A little later, Bill and Big Bob rode in, leading the pack horses and Abe's sorrel.

They too walked to the saloon and had a couple of drinks before going to their rooms.

After stowing their gear in their rooms, they all went back downstairs and started drinking whiskey. They sat in pairs at different tables around the room.

After a few drinks, each small group made their way to the café to eat dinner.

Bill and Big Bob ate at one table, while Ned, TC, and Smokey ate at another table. After they ate, Ned spoke just loud enough for all his men to hear. "I'm going to get a haircut and shave and take a bath."

Bill leaned over and whispered, "Big Bob, I'm going to go with Ned and get cleaned up so I'll be ready for the ladies tonight. I'll see you back at the saloon."

The others decided to go straight back to the saloon and drink. Ned gave them strict orders before they left. "No getting drunk, and no trouble," he hissed. "When I finish cleaning up, we'll all meet in my room to divide up the money from the bank robbery."

CHAPTER SIX

C ard closed up his family's house, and put on his chaps, heavy coat, and gloves. He walked outside and turned up his collar to protect himself from the stiff breeze as he walked to the graves and kneeled on the ground. He began crying.

He said, "Pa, I need you watching after me. I've got your gun that symbolizes power, your hat that symbolizes knowledge, and your boots that symbolize endurance. I know you were a brave fighter in the Army, and I need some of that kind of bravery for what I have to do."

He laid his hand on the ground before speaking again.

"Mama, I'll try my best to do what you want me to do, but I'll need all the strength you can give me to get it done."

Card wiped the tears off his face and mounted his horse to head downstream of the creek where he thought the gang may have exited the water. He knew the creek bed well, and he wanted to check one particular location first.

It was an area where a rocky ledge protruded into the water. His guess was that they had left the stream at that point and used the rocks to conceal their trail.

He rode a circle around the rocky ground and saw where they had headed south toward the Sulphur River. He'd been right.

Card rode at a good pace, easily staying on their trail because it wasn't hard identifying where they had been.

His pa had taught him to watch for the small things like a broken stalk of grass, a partial hoof track, or even a cigarette butt—anything that might have looked like it had been disturbed from its natural state. He made it to the river and turned upstream, since up till this point, they had left a good trail in the soft ground. He kept moving along and noticed that now the ground was starting to get harder. It might be more difficult to follow the tracks from here, thought Card. He stopped and looked around, searching for their trail, which seemed to have gone cold on the hardened earth.

If I wanted to hide my trail, here is where I would do it.

Removing the looking glass out of his saddlebag, he scanned the terrain upstream, but he couldn't make out the trail in that direction. He turned the glass south and then southwest. As he turned to look northwest, something caught his attention.

It was a small limb on a sapling that appeared to be broken. Card turned the horses toward the broken branch and rode slowly, trying to pick up the trail again. The ground got softer and the horse tracks were easy to follow once more.

Based on what he'd seen so far, he figured they were probably heading to Paris, Texas, to hole up for a spell and have a good time.

He kept wondering how they could live with themselves after what they had done to his family. They must be truly awful men that put no value on life at all, he reckoned.

The trail led into a gulley, where he found the remains of a camp from the night before. The coals in the fire were still a little warm so he decided to continue on instead of making camp. He knew his horses were tired, but he needed to make up time. He rode until it was too dark to see their trail anymore, then stopped to rest the horses and cook something to eat.

He now was almost certain they were headed to Paris. Or maybe one of the smaller towns nearby.

When his supper was over, he cleaned up his cooking utensils and plate. He decided to put out his fire and continue on, hoping he was close to finding them. He wanted to ride a few more hours before bedding down.

Two hours later he found another good place to camp in a grove of trees with fresh water and grass. There he unsaddled his horses and rubbed them down with handfuls of grass before leading them to the water's edge where he tied them so they could graze and drink.

It was unusually cold, so he didn't take any clothes off, not even his boots. A few times during the night, he awoke and thought he saw his mama coming toward him, but every time he reached out to her, he couldn't touch her. He woke up covered in sweat, realized he was dreaming, and started to cry as he huddled up in his bedroll.

Warm under his cover at first light, he didn't want to get up and face the cold air. Thoughts began to race through his mind once more.

I am getting close, and I need to be ready all the time in case I meet up with them. I sure hope I've got the courage to go through with killing them.

Finally, he threw back his covers, got up, and stretched and rubbed his eyes before looking around his campsite. He saw a thin column of smoke to the east. A lump formed in his throat and his heart began to beat quicker, thinking it could be the men he was trailing. He walked to the edge of the tree line for a better view.

He could see a town to the east. Walking quickly back to his camp, he saddled up his horses, loaded all his gear, and started toward the town. As he approached its outskirts, he saw a sign that read, *Reno, Texas*.

CHAPTER SEVEN

C ard rode down the main street of Reno, Texas. It was located six miles east of Paris, on the main road from Clarksville, Texas to Sherman, Texas. Only a few lights were on in some of the buildings since it was still before dawn. The street was mostly empty of people. Stopping at the livery stable, he found the owner already awake and tending to his chores. "Can I get my horses fed some grain, watered, and looked after for a little while?" he asked the man.

The man looked at Card, and then at his animals. "It'll be two bits for the feed, and one bit for looking after the horses," he said.

"That's all right with me. Say, is there someplace open where I can get something to eat?"

"Miss Bessie's is open," said the man, taking Smoke's reins as Card dismounted. "The food is good and the coffee's hot."

"That's all I need to know," said Card, smiling gratefully.

He walked down the street to the café and went in. There were tables with checkered cloths, and long benches to sit on.

There were only a few patrons eating breakfast at that hour, so he took a seat in the corner by himself.

A matronly-looking woman came over where he was setting. "I'm Miss Bessie. Welcome, son. What would you like this morning? I've got fresh ham, eggs, and biscuits."

"All that sounds good," replied Card. "I'd like six eggs, if that's all right, and some coffee to drink."

"Sure, that's all right," she said and left his table to return with a tin cup filled to the brim with fragrant, hot coffee.

He sat alone sipping his coffee and trying to warm up when the town marshal came in and took a seat at a nearby table with some other men.

Miss Bessie brought the marshal a steaming cup of coffee and asked, "Marshal, have you caught the crooks that robbed the bank last night and stole my money?"

"No, I haven't, but I'm working on it," said the marshal.

Miss Bessie made a disgusted face, rolling her eyes. She turned toward the kitchen door.

Card looked at the table of men drinking their coffee.

This may be a big break for me.

He got up, took his cup of coffee, and walked to the marshal's table.

"Excuse me, Marshal, my name is Card Jordon."

Without standing up, the marshal extended his hand and said, "I'm Marshal Caleb Walker."

"It's my pleasure, Marshal Walker," said Card.

Motioning to his right, the marshal introduced Card to the other men. "This is Ralph and this other man across from me is George," he said.

Card extended his hand to both the men. "It's nice to meet you fellers."

"What can I do for you, son?" the marshal asked.

"Sir," said Card, "I'm trailing five murderers and thieves that killed my family and stole some of our horses. I trailed them to right outside of town, and they may be the thieves that robbed your bank."

That seemed to get the attention of all the men at the table.

"What do you know about these men?" asked Marshal Walker as he began blowing on the hot coffee before taking a drink.

"The leader wears black clothes and carries a pearl-handled pistol. He's a cold-blooded murderer and thief," replied Card.

Marshal Walker stopped blowing on his coffee to look up at Card. "Well, I'll be John Brown. That's the same description of a stranger that came into the bank yesterday evening to get change for a hundred-dollar bill."

He motioned for Miss Bessie to come over and said to her, "Keep my coffee warm for me. I've got to go to my office and look for something." He got up and hurried out the door.

She had a surprised look on her face and so did

Ralph and George. She picked up his coffee cup and took it back into the kitchen.

Card went back to his table and sat down and continued to drink his coffee.

Miss Bessie brought Card his food and set it before him. "You sure got that old goat in an uproar a while ago," she said. "He ain't moved that fast in years."

Card smiled at her remark and started eating his food as she walked away.

The breakfast was hot and delicious, and Card wolfed it down. Then he sat back and drank another cup of coffee.

"Young man, where are you from?" asked Ralph from the other table.

"I'm from southwest Red River County, just north of Possum Trot," replied Card.

"Did we hear you right?" asked Ralph. "Those men killed your family?"

"Yeah, you heard right," replied Card.

"Are you going to take them on all by yourself?" asked George.

Taking a sip of the hot coffee, Card looked at the men. "Yeah, and I plan on killing each one of them."

Marshal Walker came back in and sat down with Card. He handed him a wanted poster and asked, "Does this description fit the person you were telling me about?"

The wanted poster was for Ned Black, wanted dead or alive with a $10,000 reward for bringing him in. It said the men he was riding with could be Big Bob Kennon, TC Stewart, Smokey Thomas, and Bill Hill.

"Yep, this is the man and the gang that I'm looking for," said Card.

"I've got wanted posters on every one of them."

Miss Bessie brought the marshal's coffee back to him and he ordered his breakfast. "I'll notify the rangers in Fort Worth about Ned Black and his gang being in the area and that they were most likely the ones that robbed our bank."

Ralph spoke up from across the room. "Marshal, are you going to put together a posse and go after those men?"

Marshal Walker slapped the table. "Now what kind of a question is that, Ralph? You know darn well I ain't got no jurisdiction outside the city limits."

"Sorry, Marshal, I didn't mean to upset you," said Ralph. "I thought we could help."

Miss Bessie brought the marshal his food and placed it in front of him and he started eating.

"Marshal, how far is it to Paris?" asked Card. "I've a good mind they're going there to hole up for a while and spend some of that money they stole from the bank."

Marshal Walker spoke with a mouthful of food. "Card, it's six miles to Paris. Just follow the train tracks."

"Thank you, sir," said Card, getting up from the table. He paid for his meal and left the café.

He went back to the livery stable and collected his horses.

The stable hand came over and said, "Your dapple gray has a loose shoe on his right rear hoof. 'Iffin I was you, I would take him over to the blacksmith right now and have it looked after, because you sure don't want to throw a shoe on the trail and take the risk of him coming up lame."

Card thought about that. Then he said, "Thanks, I believe I'll do just that."

He took hold of Smoke's bridle reins and walked him to the blacksmith shop.

The blacksmith, who was replacing spokes in a wagon wheel, looked up as Card approached. "What can I do for you?"

"My horse is about to throw a shoe, and I need it looked after," replied Card.

"All right, tie your horse over by the water trough and I'll get started on him in an hour or so."

"Much obliged," said Card. "I'm going to Marshal Walker's office in case you need me for anything."

"Sure thing," said the blacksmith, without looking up from his work.

Card walked into Marshal Walker's office to find him sitting at his desk, looking at the wanted posters of Ned and his gang.

"Howdy Card, I thought you were leaving?"

"I was, but my horse has a loose shoe," said Card. "Marshal, can I have those wanted papers on the outlaws that robbed the bank and killed my family?"

"No, these are the only posters I've got on these fellows, and I'd hate to give them away," responded the marshal.

"I understand. I thought you might have more than one set."

"Young man, what do you plan to do when you catch up to these men?" Marshal Walker asked.

"I am going to kill each and every one of them," said Card. He looked at Marshal Walker with a determined face.

"I don't blame you," said Marshal Walker. "But here's my advice, whether you want it or not. You make sure that you kill them in self-defense because it'd be a shame if you got in trouble over killing the likes of them."

"Thanks, Marshal, for the advice," said Card. "I think I'll walk to the mercantile and stock up on some provisions while my horse is getting tended to. You have a nice day."

"You too, Card. Be careful."

Card nodded and left the marshal's office. He walked to the store and bought a few items: Jerky, coffee, and pickled eggs.

He went back to the blacksmith shop to check on the man's progress and tie the sack of new items onto his saddle.

Smoke was still tied up in the same place as he had left him. Card was getting a little aggravated by the blacksmith's slow pace. But there was nothing that could be done, so he decided to see if he could get a haircut and a bath while he waited. He walked to the barbershop and made arrangements for a hot bath in thirty minutes, then walked across the street to a dry goods store and bought some new clothes. He went back to the barbershop for his haircut and was able to get right in the chair. This was his first haircut from anyone other than his mama, and just the thought of her made his eyes moisten up.

After the haircut, he walked into the back room of

the barbershop and got in the tub of hot water that had been prepared for him. He was overdue for a good bath, and it sure made him feel better.

Card put on his new clothes, combed his freshly cut hair, and returned once again to the blacksmith's shop.

The blacksmith had finished with Smoke, and Card paid him for the work done. Then he rode back to the stable to get his pack horse.

Since it was past noon, Card decided to eat dinner before leaving town. He no longer felt like he was in a big hurry; the murderous gang was probably laid up in Paris for a few days, having fun and thinking no one was on to them.

Miss Bessie had beef stew and cornbread for dinner. Card ate a big bowl of food and drank four cups of coffee before paying for his meal and going back to the livery stable.

He made sure his supplies were secured to the pack saddle and left Reno at two-thirty in the afternoon, taking the road alongside the railroad right-of-way toward Paris.

Card watched the countryside go by from the saddle of his horse and let his mind wander. With the railroad so close to town, he reasoned, it would be nice to have cattle pens and loading docks near the train station, as there didn't seem to be any way to get cattle on a train. That way, all the ranchers in the area could bring their cattle right to the station and have them shipped to market, instead of making cattle drives to Kansas. And whoever built those pens and loading docks could become a wealthy man. What if that man was him?

His mind wandered further. Would the railroad give him a contract for the pens? And maybe he could buy more land and cattle himself, to take advantage of easier shipping. He vowed to give it more thought… when his promise to his mama had been fulfilled.

It was dusty dark when he pulled up at the first livery stable he could find.

"Would you feed my horses some grain and water, and put them in a stall for the night?" Card asked the livery owner. "And would it be okay if I slept in your hayloft?"

"Yep, you can use the hayloft, but it will cost you six bits for everything."

Card paid the man, grabbed his bedroll, travel bag, and rifle, and climbed up the ladder to the loft.

CHAPTER EIGHT

Ned and Bill finished cleaning up, having gotten a haircut, shave, and a hot bath, before heading back to the saloon and up the stairs to Ned's room.

They'd seen the rest of the men sitting at the bar, and Ned gave a subtle nod for them to follow in a few minutes.

When he got to his room, Ned pulled the sack of cash out of his saddlebags and waited for the others to arrive. It wasn't long until there was a knock on the door.

Bill pulled his gun and stood to the side of the door while Ned opened it and invited the other three men into the room. They stood watching as Ned dumped the money on the bed.

"Bill, you and TC count the money and the rest of us will watch," he said.

They counted $13,440.

Ned pulled a pencil and paper out of his bag and

ciphered out how much each man's share was. It came to $2,666 each.

Bill was the most excited. He yelped, "I'm going to have ever' working girl in this place before I leave!"

Ned laughed. "I want you all to leave this room one at a time and don't sit together in the saloon. We need to act like strangers to each other for a day or so."

They returned to the saloon and drank until late that night.

Ned woke up the next day to the sounds of a busy, industrious town. He could hear hammers and saws building new structures and wagons rattling down the street.

Throwing the covers off, Ned got up, washed his face, combed his hair, and got dressed. He left his room and went downstairs and out the door, where he stood taking in the sights of a busy little city as people hustled along doing their business.

He smiled. This could turn into a very productive place for him and his men, what with all the new money in town financing the new businesses under construction. He was sure the banks were holding substantial reserves to meet the construction demands. He made a mental note to start checking out the banks and develop a plan for a robbery or two.

Something caught his eye as he walked toward the café. Across the street was a billboard where wanted posters and city information were posted for everyone to see.

He crossed the street and walked up to the posters. Lo and behold, there was a wanted poster with his name on it, and posters on each of his gang members.

After he looked up and down the street, he reached up and tore the posters off the board. He grew red-faced and fumed because the picture didn't look anything like him. And it was only a $10,000 reward! This was bad, thought Ned. The posters might put a damper on his plans to rob a bank here. He folded the posters up and put them in his pocket. Trying to get his anger under control, he turned and went back across the street, moving swiftly toward the café.

After observing the city and wanting to stay here a few days and check out the banks, Ned knew this was a problem that wasn't going to go away. Maybe a good meal would help him think better. In the café, he took a seat alone and was lost in thought when a waitress came to his table to take his order. He asked for a cup of coffee with his meal while he waited, he thought about what to do next. When his food arrived, he tucked into the plateful of food and began to develop a plan. He knew what they needed to do.

After the meal, he walked back to the saloon where he found Smokey and TC standing at the bar drinking coffee laced with whiskey.

Ned told them about the posters. "I want the two of you, along with Bill, to ride on to Honey Grove," said Ned. "It's about twenty-two miles to the west. Hold up there. It's less than a day's ride so if you leave now, you can be there before dark. I'll stay here and help Big Bob sell those horses, then we'll meet up with you guys."

"Aw," said Smokey. "I was hopin' I'd be the one to stay, I got my eye on one of them ladies over there."

He jerked his head to a group of three women seated by the window.

"Well, that's just too bad, you're going," said Ned.

TC slapped Smokey on the back, causing him to spill some of his drink. "Smoke, I'm sure there'll be women lined up waiting for you when you get to Honey Grove."

"Shut up, TC, you done made me spill my drink," said Smokey.

"Pay attention, you two," said Ned while raising his voice. "The law at Honey Grove isn't really strict on who comes into town as long as they don't cause him no trouble and line his pockets every now and then."

"That all sounds fine, but you need to tell Bill to come with us yourself. You know he don't like taking orders from me," said TC.

Tapping the countertop, Ned motioned for the barkeep that he wanted a drink. "Okay, I'll talk to Bill." The man slid a glass down the bar top and Ned knocked it back in one big swallow.

"Thanks, Ned," said TC. "You know Bill can be difficult when you're not around."

"Just remember," Ned went on, "Honey Grove is a small farming town where we can lay low a few days and maybe have some fun, but make sure no one draws any attention to us there by getting into trouble."

TC nodded and Smokey said, "Sure thing, boss."

A few minutes later, all three men went upstairs to tell the other men what was going on. "We're moving on to Honey Grove," explained Ned, pulling the crumpled wanted posters out of his pocket. He told his men about the plan for everyone to head out except for him and Big Bob.

"I pulled these off the billboard outside," said Ned. "It's just a matter of time before someone recognizes one of us and the law comes calling. So, start packing up your things and do what TC says until I get there. Bill, do you understand?"

"Yeah, I understand," replied Bill.

Ned looked at Big Bob. "We need to sell all the horses before me and you can leave here. We'll be faster if we don't have to lead horses all the time. Don't draw any attention to yourself trying to sell them, got it? If we don't make it to Honey Grove until tomorrow, that'll be fine, the others will still be there waiting on us."

Big Bob scratched his beard. "Ned, ain't you coming with me to sell the horses?"

Ned wanted to say something rude to Big Bob but didn't. "Yeah, Bob, I'll go with you to sell the horses." Ned changed his mind because he knew Big Bob had difficulty talking to strangers.

Smokey took a step closer to Big Bob and looked up at his bearded face. "Bob, don't you go bedding my woman since I'm having to leave."

Big Bob started laughing and hugged Smokey. "Don't you worry one bit, Smokey. I'll watch over her real good for you."

Ned smiled. "You fellers get going so you can be there before dark."

Bill, Smokey, and TC packed up and headed to the livery stable to get their horses and leave town.

CHAPTER NINE

The sun came through the cracks in the walls and woke Card up from his night of sleeping in the hayloft. After rubbing the sleep from his eyes, he got up and rolled up his bedroll and tossed it and his travel bag to the ground below. After he climbed down the ladder, he put all of his supplies together and left them in a corner of the barn. Next, he checked on his horses and then went outside.

He was amazed by what he saw. In the light of day, he realized Paris was the biggest town he had ever seen. There was a diner across the street, so he went and ordered breakfast. The food was delicious, and he ate a good-sized meal.

He decided to saddle Smoke and ride down Main Street and around the square to look at all the shops, stores, and businesses, because it seemed there was a store for about anything a person might need. He also wanted to talk to a few local ranchers.

He rode around town and stopped at a feed store,

where he went in and talked to some of the men and asked them how many head of cattle they owned, and if they'd be interested in shipping their livestock to eastern markets from a local location as opposed to making cattle drives into Kansas. Everyone he talked to was intrigued by the idea. He felt like he might be onto something and told himself he'd definitely look into making a plan for the future.

Card left the feed store and stopped at a gun shop to look at all the new pistols and to purchase two boxes of .44 caliber shells.

After stowing the bullets in his saddlebags, Card mounted back up and continued through town. A quick glance to his left, revealed another livery stable tucked down a side street. Pulling back on the reins, he stopped Smoke abruptly. In the holding pen were Pa's sorrel stallion and the two broodmares.

He took the safety thong off his gun and rode to the stable door where he dismounted. The stable hand came out to greet Card and asked, "What can I help you with?"

Card motioned to the sorrel. "Do you know anything about that stud horse?"

"He's for sale and so are those two mares over there." He pointed to the holding pens.

"Do you know if the owner is around?" asked Card.

"Yep, he's probably across the street at the saloon. Two men brought them in yesterday, but one of them has already left town.

"Can you describe the man at the saloon for me?"

Card felt anxiety fill his belly as he realized he might be closer to the killers than he'd thought.

"Yes sir," said the stable hand. "He's a big man, about your height. Probably weighs around three hundred pounds, and he's got a dirty beard and wears a red and white checkered shirt."

"Thanks," said Card. He turned to walk away but stopped and looked back. "That man killed my family and stole those horses, so I'm going over there and give him his due, then I'm coming back for what's mine."

"Yessir, I understand," said the stable hand in a frightened voice.

Card turned and continued to the saloon. Thoughts about what he would do when he came face-to-face with the murderers was on his mind. What would he do it they were all together? He would kill the leader first. He deliberately made himself walk slowly to keep his awareness sharp and attentive and not let the rage that was built up inside of him control his actions. He was on a well-thought-out mission to kill some men.

Card pushed through the batwing doors and stepped to the side, giving his eyes time to adjust to the darkness.

He surveyed the room, scanning each person. Sitting over by the piano was Big Bob who was eating a huge meal. He had food in his beard and on the front of his shirt. A disgusting sight, thought Card. He must be alone; he didn't see any of the others in the room.

Card turned and walked back outside. He was so nervous that he could hear his heart beating. He stood out on the sidewalk breathing in deep breaths of air and thought about his dead family shot to death by that hideous man sitting in the saloon. He knew without a doubt that he was fast and could beat the slob at the table to the draw. He let his hatred and rage give him strength and confidence as he turned and walked back into the saloon.

Card remembered the man's name from the wanted poster. He approached the table where Big Bob sat eating like a pig, when he was within hearing distance of the man, Card stopped. He absent-mindedly rubbed his fingers and thumb together on his gun hand.

"Big Bob, you murdering, stealing scum," said Card. "You killed my family and stole my pa's horses, and it's time you pay your dues and die."

Bob kicked his chair back and spewed food on the table as he stood up. He was fuming mad. He shouted, "No one talks to me this way and lives, especially some snot-nosed kid!"

He had an expression of rage on his face as he dropped his hand to his side and went for his gun. Big Bob was fast for a big man, but he was no match for the youngster standing in front of him who was full of hate and revenge.

It was the last mistake Big Bob Kennan ever made.

Card let his instincts take over as his hand flashed to the gun and pulled it from the holster before Big Bob could even come close to bringing his own gun into play.

Card put two bullets in the middle of Big Bob's chest. The big man took a step backward while looking down at the blood oozing out of his chest. His expression changed to shock and confusion and his eyes glazed over. Bob tried to raise his gun, but nothing was working. He collapsed onto the table, shattering it as he fell to the floor, dead.

The patrons in the saloon were murmuring about the gunman and one of the saloon girls had fainted.

CHAPTER TEN

Ned heard the shooting from his room; two quick shots. He had been enjoying the company of one of the saloon girls, and he told her to stay put as he grabbed his gun and went out the door onto the balcony where he looked down to see what was going on.

He saw Big Bob sprawled out on the floor, and standing over Bob was a young man, reloading bullets into a gun.

Ned fired a shot at him but missed because of his angle from the balcony. Card turned, closed the chamber on his gun and fired two shots. One hit Ned, grazing his arm.

"Dammit, he hit me." He jumped back and ran back to his room.

Card started up the stairs after him when he heard a voice hollering, "Halt!"

The town marshal was behind him with his gun drawn and pointed right at him, so he stopped.

The marshal said, "Ease that gun down to the floor real slow, and no fast moves."

Card bent down, never taking his eyes off the marshal, and placed his gun on the floor.

He stood up with his hands in plain sight. "My name is Card Jordon. Me and my family live on the southwest side of Red River County, about four miles northwest of the settlement of Possum Trot. Four days ago, this scum and four other men murdered my family and stole our horses. The one upstairs is the leader, and if you check your wanted posters, you'll find paper on each one of them."

With the gun down to his side, the marshal walked to where Big Bob lay. He spoke in a loud voice so the people in the room could hear. "I don't want no one leaving until I can get a statement, is that understood?"

The bar customers nodded their heads in acknowledgment.

After his initial survey of the body, he turned back to Card.

"I'm Marshal Dover." He pointed with his gun at a nearby chair. "You can go over to that table and take a seat while I finish my investigation."

"But Marshal, that other feller is getting away," Card tried to argue with the man. "I need to go after him."

"Young man, first things first. You have a seat and be quiet until I finish getting statements, is that clear?"

Card nodded reluctantly. He was fuming and wanted to go after Ned, but knew he had to obey the law.

Marshal Dover took a seat at one of the tables and told the barkeep he needed a pencil and paper.

The marshal raised his hand to get everyone's attention and addressed the whole saloon.

"I want any of you that saw what happened, come over here and give me your statement."

After he had written down each person's testimony, he had them sign or put their mark on the paper.

Next the marshal searched Big Bob's pockets and found his money.

Card stood up to speak. "Marshal, that money was stolen from the bank in Reno and needs to be returned."

Marshal Dover retorted, "Okay, but first you follow me to my office and we'll see if there's a wanted poster on this man. In the meantime, I'll hold on to your gun until we get there."

They walked out the door of the saloon. "My office is to your right and down the sidewalk a short distance."

They made a quick stop at the undertaker's place of business to notify him about the body.

Once at the jailhouse, they went through the wanted posters and sure enough, found papers on all five men.

"Card, I'll send a wire for the reward money and when it gets here, you're free to go," said Marshal Dover. "But I'd appreciate it if you don't cause any more trouble while you're here."

He handed Card his gun back.

"Give me some paper and I'll write down the name

of the bank my pa uses in Clarksville, Texas, and you can have the money sent there since I need to get on my way before the trail grows cold," said Card.

The door opened and in walked the Lamar County sheriff, Sheriff Pete Gose. He introduced himself to Card and they shook hands.

Marshal Dover filled the sheriff in on the shooting and what Card had told him about the gang killing his family. The sheriff listened to it all, and then he said, "I'll send a telegram to the other towns in the county telling them to be on the lookout for Ned and his gang. I was notified by the rangers yesterday that they could be in the area."

"I appreciate the work that both of you do, but I need to get going," said Card. "Hopefully the next time we meet, it will not involve a shooting." He stood to leave.

Marshal Dover and Sheriff Gose shook Card's hand and wished him well.

"I'm sorry about your family, and hope you find all the killers," said Sheriff Gose. "You be careful. These are some mean, unscrupulous men, and they won't think twice about bushwhacking you on the trail somewhere."

"Thanks for the advice, sheriff," said Card.

CHAPTER ELEVEN

After he got shot, Ned ran back to his room, clutching his arm in pain. "Here, take this handkerchief and tie it around my arm where that snot-nosed kid shot me." While the saloon girl covered his wound, he heard someone holler, "Halt!" downstairs. He knew he had little time to escape, so he picked up his coat and grabbed a few of his things to take with him. He didn't have any backup, since all his men had gone to Honey Grove. He needed to get away before the town law came looking for him. The saloon girl opened the door and looked down the hallway; it was clear so she motioned for Ned and he hurried toward the back stairway and out the back door. When he was outside, he ran toward the livery stable.

There he saddled his horse and started out of town. But an idea came to him, and he decided to change course.

Ned turned in behind the row of buildings across

the street from the saloon and rode until he was directly across from the bar. He left his horse in the alley and eased as close as he could to the street, staying in the shadows.

He got his rifle ready to shoot and his finger rested lightly on the trigger as he waited in the obscurities.

Card and Marshal Dover came out of the saloon together and walked up the sidewalk. Ned didn't have a clear shot and couldn't chance a shootout with the law, so he backed away to his horse and headed toward Honey Grove. His chance at the young gunman would have to wait.

CHAPTER TWELVE

C ard left the marshal's office and walked to the livery stable to get his horses ready to travel. "Have you seen a man here with blood on his shirt this morning?" he asked the stable hand.

"No sir, but there was a man here about an hour ago getting his horse, and he sure was favoring his left arm. Like it was hurt or something," said the boy. "He was in a big hurry to get out of here, from what I could tell."

Card mounted his horse and checked that everything was secured to the saddle. "Can you describe him to me?"

"Yes sir, he was dressed in black clothes and had a fancy gun. Was he in on that ruckus over at the saloon?"

"Yeah, and he's a dangerous man," replied Card. "Do you know which way he was headed?"

The stable hand pointed and said, "Yep, he left that there way over yonder between those buildings. He stayed there for about ten minutes or so then he took off heading west like he was being chased by a grizzly bear."

"Much obliged," said Card. "That sorrel and those two mares in the holding pen are mine and I want to board them here until I can get back to collect them."

The stable hand looked at the horses Card was referring to. "I'll take good care of them for you," he said. "It'll be thirty dollars to keep them for a month."

"That's agreeable," said Card, and handed the man thirty dollars out of his pocket. "If it takes a little longer than a month for me to get back, don't sell them. I wouldn't appreciate that!"

The stableman got the hint and replied, "Oh no sir, I'll take good care of your horses and they'll be here when you get back, I guarantee."

Card walked his horse away from the stable and in the direction the boy said Ned had gone.

He had no trouble picking up the tracks from the point where Ned had left his horse in the alley. He followed Ned's boot tracks to where he had stood watching the street. It was easy to figure out what he'd been trying to do.

Card went back to his horse, and once again picked up Ned's tracks heading west out of town. He could tell that Ned's horse had been in a full run and had torn up the ground with its hooves.

A quarter mile west of Paris, the tracks merged onto a road and seemed to continue on west. Card knew it would be almost impossible to follow the tracks any longer because the road was so well-used. He decided to push on and see where the road went.

He rode hard for another ten miles until the light was beginning to dim. It was time for him to find a good campsite for the night.

Up by Tanyard Creek, he turned upstream and followed a trail, looking for someplace to stop where there was some shelter from the cold. Fifty yards farther on, he found an abandoned camp that looked like it hadn't been used in a while. But there was grass nearby, and he could see where travelers had watered their horses.

CHAPTER THIRTEEN

N ed rode his horse hard and was still boiling mad about getting shot and then missing the young guy that had shot Big Bob in the saloon.

He'd been taught bushwhacking from the best—Bill Anderson. Bill was given the name of Bloody Bill because he killed countless innocent men, women, and children during the Civil War while riding with Quantrill's raiders.

Ned searched for the optimal spot to hold up and wait on the gunman. He came to a bridge over a small creek and stopped to examine the area to see if it might be the right place to kill the man.

A trail to the north looked like a path travelers used to get their horses down to the water to drink. He rode across the bridge and found a location where he could conceal his horse. While searching along the creek bank, he saw two trees growing side-by-side where he could conceal himself and have a good field of fire across the creek and bridge.

He had been taught to get comfortable and have patience. It could be a long wait sometimes. But at the same time, he needed to be in position and ready to fire quickly.

Ned stood behind two trees with his rifle aimed, watching as Card rode down the trail toward the water. It looked like he was searching for a place to camp for the night.

Carefully taking aim, Ned pulled the trigger. He felt the gun buck in his hand and watched the gunman twist in the saddle from the impact of the bullet as it hit him.

He watched as the man pulled his gun and started firing blindly into the trees along the creek.

Ned fired a second shot and saw the man on the horse tumble from the saddle and onto the ground. He stood watching with his rifle aimed and ready to shoot again. He could see blood on the side of the gunman's head and face, and the figure was not moving. Ned smiled with confidence and walked to his horse where he mounted and then rode back across the bridge to where the man was lying. The figure was still in the same position as before. There was blood on his head and face, and blood on his shoulder. Ned pulled his gun, about to make sure the man was good and dead, but heard someone coming down the road so he took off up the creek.

CHAPTER FOURTEEN

N ed stayed off the road for about a mile then continued on toward Honey Grove.

He arrived at the livery stable just after dark and told the stable hand to take care of his horse as he handed him a dollar.

As he was leaving, Ned saw his men's horses in the corral. "Do you know where the owners of those horses might happen to be?" he asked.

"I saw them go into the café, so they are most likely eating supper at this time of day." The man pointed across the street.

Ned went across the street to the café where Bill, Smokey and TC were eating supper. He pulled up a chair and ordered a plate of food while Bill eyed him with a frown on his face, as if waiting for Ned to share some news.

"Big Bob is dead," said Ned in a low voice. "He was gunned down in the saloon back in Paris by some young wannabe quickdraw."

They all responded with a shocked look on their faces.

"Well, tell us exactly what happened," said Bill.

"Let's finish eating and then we'll talk about it outside where no one can hear us," Ned told them.

After supper they left the café and walked back toward the boarding house where they had rented rooms. Ned stopped in a secluded location between two buildings, right before they got to the house.

Smokey rolled himself a cigarette and lit it, waiting for Ned to tell his story.

"Big Bob was in the saloon," Ned said. "I was upstairs in my room when I heard two quick shots. I grabbed my gun and went to the balcony and looked down to see Big Bob sprawled out on the floor, dead as a doornail. I fired at the gunman but missed. He fired at me and grazed my left arm. Then I went to my room and grabbed my things and snuck out the back door. I was going to take another shot at him, but the law was there too, so I hightailed it right on out of there."

TC shifted from one leg to the other. "Do you know who the gunman was?"

"No, I've never seen him before, and I'll never see him again," said Ned. "I waited on him at the creek—the one that has a bridge over it. I found me a good spot with a good view and waited until he came along. At which time I put two bullets in him and left him for the buzzards to feed on."

Smokey blew out a column of smoke. "Do you suspect he was a bounty hunter after us for the reward money?"

Ned scratched his chin. "I don't know, but we

don't have to look over our shoulders for him no more since I took care of that. It's just too bad that Big Bob had to die. He was with me longer than any of you, and I could always depend on him in a fight."

"Yep, that's too bad," said Bill.

"What's bad is, I couldn't get his money off him for the rest of us to have fun with," said Ned. "Now the law has it. But we're alive and there's plenty more money to be taken here in Honey Grove."

Smokey removed the cigarette from his lips and threw the butt to the ground. "I say we go to the saloon and have a toast to Big Bob."

TC slapped Smokey on the back. "Smokey, that's the best idea you've had in a while."

They were underway to the saloon when Ned stopped in his tracks. "Smokey, you and Bill go on ahead. Me and TC will follow up in a few minutes."

CHAPTER FIFTEEN

C ard dreamed he was with his family, laughing and talking with them, telling them about finding Big Bob. He felt no remorse at all for killing Big Bob, and as he lay looking up at the sky, he smiled and said, "Mama, I got the first one." Then the blackness overtook him again.

It started to rain, during the night; a slow cold rain that would chill even the heartiest man to the bone.

Card woke up around three in the morning soaking wet, extremely cold and feeling like he had been run over by a herd of cattle. He had a terrible headache, and it was difficult to move his shoulder for the pain. He was so cold that he was shaking and thought he must have a fever.

All I need right now is to get sick out here on the trail without any shelter or medicine.

He tried to sit up, but he went back into unconsciousness.

By the time daylight came it was raining harder

and the wind was blowing. Card managed to get up and stand on weak legs while holding on to a tree. His head was hurting and throbbing, so he reached up and ran his fingers along the left side of his skull, finding a deep slash in his scalp. After examining the gash with his fingers, he looked at his hand and saw blood. He also had pain in his left shoulder that was so bad that he could hardly move his arm. He stood and tried to focus on where he was and what had happened to him. It was all still a bit hazy, but memories of the sound of a rifle started to return and he realized he had been shot. He needed to find his horse and go get help; he didn't want to die in the middle of nowhere all alone.

As his senses slowly come back to him, he could hear his horse nearby. He turned carefully and saw Smoke eating grass a few feet away.

Card had a hard time getting in the saddle. He kept falling backward whenever he tried to put his foot in the stirrup and hoist himself onto the horse's back. He looked for a foothold to help him get mounted and found a nearby log. He led his horse to it and climbed onto the log to put his foot in the stirrup. With much effort, he hoisted himself up enough to finally get in the saddle after three attempts.

He sat for a moment and waited until he could focus again and his breathing quieted down.

When he felt like he could manage it, he took hold of the reins and walked Smoke over to his packhorse. He almost fell out of the saddle when he reached for the lead rope. Grabbing the pommel for support, he got the rope and tied it to his saddle horn.

Card finally got back to the road and headed across the bridge toward Honey Grove.

It felt like he'd caught two bullets based on the pain in his arm and the side of his head. He needed a doctor, bad.

As he rode, he leaned over the saddle horn, trying to keep the constant rain off him.

Shivers from his fever racked his body and he was in shock from the bullet wounds. Darkness kept invading his thoughts, and he knew he was slipping in and out of consciousness.

Mama, I need you to help me. If only there was some shelter where I could get out of the cold.

Just then, Card spotted a light through the trees just off the road; it had to be a house. He would ask if they could give him shelter in their barn. He rode into the yard and hollered for help as loud as he could, but no one came to the door. He pulled his gun out and fired a shot into the sky.

An elderly man slowly opened the door, holding a shotgun.

"Sir, I mean you no harm," Card said. "I'm real sick and need shelter to get out of this weather." An older woman joined the man at the door. She asked, "Sonny, what's wrong with you?"

"Ma'am, I've been shot, and I've got a fever and feel terrible bad, I'm so cold," said Card as he hunched shivering over the horn of his saddle.

"Get down off that horse and get in the house you need tending to," she said.

Card tried to dismount and fell to the ground, landing in the water and mud.

The old man came out and lifted him up, then put his arm around the boy's waist and helped him in the house.

"Take him to the kitchen and set him down, and then go get me a quilt to put around him," the old woman said. "Son, what's your name?"

"I'm Card Jordon," he replied through trembling lips.

The old woman took a seat beside Card. "I'm Sue Marshall and this is my husband, Jacob Marshall. Jacob, go get the bottle."

She pointed to the living room, and Jacob left the room. She got up and took a glass off the shelf of dishes and put some honey in it. Jacob brought her the bottle of whiskey and poured some in the glass along with the honey. Then he took a spoon, stirred it up, and handed it to Card. "You drink this down."

"Jacob, take his horses to the barn, and unsaddle them and give them some feed. You can bring his gear in so we can see if he has any dry clothes," said Sue.

Card drank down the entire toddy. It was strong with whiskey and tasted terrible and made him a little lightheaded. But it seemed to warm his belly some.

A girl came into the kitchen and eyed Card curiously. Sue said, "This is Jean, she's our granddaughter and lives with us. Jean, this young man is Card, he's been shot and has a fever and we're going to look after him for a while."

Looking up at Jean, Card smiled. "Hi, you're very pretty."

Her mouth fell open and she blushed at his remark. She lowered her head to hide the red glow to her face. "Grandma, I think there is something wrong with his eyes also."

It took all his strength to hold his head up. "No, my eyes are just fine."

Sue touched the girl on the arm. "Go into the spare bedroom and get the mattress off the bed and take it into the living room. Then you can place it close to the fire. Oh, and then find some quilts and blankets too, because we'll have to sweat the fever out of him after I tend to his wounds."

Sue handed Card another toddy. He took a drink and set the glass on the table. "I can't drink the rest, it tastes terrible."

He felt dizzier than before, and his head was pounding. As he sat in the chair, he swayed back and forth. He was still so cold in his wet clothes, and the fever was making him shake uncontrollably.

Jacob came back in with Card's bag, and Sue went through it and found some clean clothes.

Sue brought a pan of hot water over to the table. "Jacob, hold on to him while I clean his wounds, so he doesn't fall out of the chair. This will probably hurt him, so you may need Jean to help."

Jacob called out to Jean. "Girl, come into the kitchen and help me."

Jacob held Card's upper body as Jean held his legs.

Sue took a warm rag and washed the gash on his head. The bullet had grazed the side of his skull and left a nasty cut. She went to her sewing basket and removed a piece of material long enough to go around his head, and then took a mixture of kerosene and sugar and applied it on the wound to fight infection. It burned really bad, and Card was in pain as she wrapped the material around his head to control the bleeding.

"Jean," said Sue. "Help me. We need to cut his shirt off and see about his shoulder."

Jacob held Card in the chair as Jean and Sue cut his shirt off. The bullet had gone in below the shoulder joint, through muscle and fat.

"It's good that the bullet went clean through," said Jacob.

Next, Sue washed the bullet hole out with some of the whiskey. Card hollered out in pain as it stung his exposed flesh.

When Sue was finished dressing his wound, she said, "Me and Jean will go into another room. Jacob, you help him get changed into clean dry clothes, then we'll all help get him to his bed on the living room floor. I think that shot to the head is going to affect his balance for a while, so we need to hold him when he gets up."

All that whiskey he had drunk was making him drowsy. It was hard for him to stay awake as Jacob helped him into his clean clothes. Finally, he lay down on the bed that Jean had made for him close to the fire, and Sue covered him up.

Card had a rough night. He kept waking up freezing, sweating, and talking out of his head and hallucinating. Sue got up once and made him another hot toddy to help him sleep. He drank it down and went back into a deep sleep while she stayed up wiping sweat off his face and chest with a cold towel.

When it was daylight, Jacob built up the fire in the

cookstove and put on water to boil for coffee. Card noticed Jean was up; he watched her as she went into the kitchen to cook breakfast with Sue.

Card sat up and looked around, confused about where he was.

He looked at Jacob. "Where am I, and what's happened to me?"

"Don't you remember when you got here last night and what happened to you yesterday?"

Card thought for a few seconds and said, "Yes sir, I do remember a little bit. I got shot and came here and you helped me into the house. And you are Jacob, and your wife is Sue."

Jacob nodded his head. "You've been shot in two places and my wife thinks you'll be dizzy for a while, so you probably shouldn't make any fast moves just yet."

"There's bacon, ham, and some canned food on my pack saddle," said Card. "When you go to the barn would you bring it back in? We need to eat it up before it turns bad."

"Sure thing," said Jacob as he made his way to the door.

Sue brought in a plate of food and set it down on a table close to the mattress. "Card, you lie there and Jean will come in here and feed this to you. I don't want you trying to sit up yet. When you're finished eating, I want you to drink another hot toddy."

"Yes, ma'am," said Card as he propped his head up with his good arm.

Jean was only able to get him to eat a few bites of the eggs and bacon; he just didn't feel like eating. He was getting cold again and his fever was coming back.

He drank the toddy she held to his lips and lay back down, and it wasn't long before he was shaking and sweating again from a high temperature.

This time Jean took over wiping the sweat off his face and caring for him. She stayed in the room and kept him covered, trying to sweat the infection out of his body.

Card reached out and took her hand and pulled her close. He smelled her hand and then he touched her hair.

Jean pushed his hand away. "What in tarnation are you doing?"

Card reached out and took her hand in his again. "I thought I was dead, and you were an angel."

Jean smiled and let him hold her hand.

Sue fixed another hot toddy for Card and brought it to Jean with instructions to give it to him slowly.

Jean put her hand under his head and helped him sit up. "I have some delicious medicine for you. Please drink it all down and I'll hold your hand some more."

He would only take little sips in between losing consciousness, but eventually she managed to get him to drink it all. He slept for three full hours without fever, only waking up about dark, needing to get to the outhouse.

Jacob bundled him up and helped him walk across the yard. He was so weak that it took all the strength he had to get back into the house, even with Jacob's aid.

Jean had a bowl of hot broth waiting for him when

he got back inside. He sat on his bed drinking it and trying to clear the cobwebs from his brain.

He was so thirsty, he needed something else to drink so she went to get him a glass of water and a cup of coffee. By the time he finished his coffee and water, he had to lie back down.

Sue came in with hot water and clean dressings. She took a look at his wounds. The flesh around them was a little red and inflamed but not too badly, so she applied some healing salve that the family used on cuts and such on their horses, and clean bandages.

It was dark now, and Sue, Jacob, and Jean sat in the living room with Card. Sue asked, "Card, why were you out in this weather, and why did you keep talking in your sleep about your mama, pa, and family?"

Card lay on his bed with tears in his eyes and a scowl on his face. He didn't want to discuss it right then.

"If you don't want to talk about it now, I understand," she said softly.

Card nodded his head, turned over, and closed his eyes.

He fell asleep and a memory came to him in his rest. He was fishing with his pa and his brother Ben. It was the time when they had been at the creek and his sisters came down to see the fish they had caught and put on a stringer. Ben had put earthworms on both his sisters' heads, and they'd run back to the house screaming. They had all laughed about it at supper that night.

Jean woke him up by holding his head up. She pleaded, "Please drink this delicious toddy, I'll hold your hand while you empty the glass. Come on now, I know you can do it."

He was able to drink it down and then fell back to sleep.

He only had a fever once that night, and the next morning he was able to get up and eat breakfast and drink coffee without getting dizzy. Even his headaches had eased up some.

It had quit raining and the sun was shining. It looked like it was going to be a beautiful day.

Sue told Jacob, "I'm almost out of whiskey for toddies and such, you need to go into town and buy some more, plus a few other things we need from the store."

"Make me a list and I'll go get it," said Jacob. "I'm goin' to go hitch up the wagon."

Card had Jean bring him his travel bag, and he felt around in it and brought out some money.

He called Sue into the room and gave her twenty-five dollars and said, "You get whatever you need, I'm paying for it."

"It ain't necessary for you to pay for everything, but I do appreciate it," said Sue. "Since we don't have much cash here at the house."

Jacob came back in the house. "Where's the list?" he asked.

"Right here," said Sue as she handed him the list and the cash Card had given her. "And Card has offered to pay."

Jacob counted the bills. "Well, That's mighty nice of you, Card."

Card gave him a wave of his hand. "It's the least I can do for you taking me in."

"Uh, excuse me, but I'm the one that's been taking care of you, Mr. Card Jordan," said Jean.

Card smiled. "Yes, you have, and you're doing a fine job, Miss Jean Marshall."

Jean laughed and turned toward Jacob. "Can I go with you, Grandpa?"

"No, you're needed here to help out," said Sue.

"Please, Grandma," said Jean. "I never get to go into town."

"Jean, you do as you're told," said Jacob.

Jean bowed her head as if disappointed to miss a chance to go window shopping.

"Mr. Marshall," said Card. "While you are in there, would you keep an eye out for a man dressed in all-black clothing and wearing a pearl-handled gun? If you see him, stay away from him, he's dangerous."

Jacob nodded and walked out the door.

This was the first time Card felt well enough to really recognize how pretty Jean was. He felt his face flush thinking about her. He hadn't been around girls before except his sisters, and they didn't count. She had reddish blond hair, a cute smile, and high cheek-bones. He thought she was very pretty and enjoyed her taking care of him. He loved her touch and how she pampered him.

Card was feeling much better. "Would it be okay for me to wash off?" he asked Sue.

He had gotten so sweaty, he figured he probably smelled bad and was embarrassed to be close to Jean and Sue.

"Go bring the washtub into the kitchen and draw some water from the well to heat so he can have a bath," Sue told Jean.

"Yes ma'am," said Jean, giving Card a quick blushing glance.

Jean brought in four buckets of water and poured them in the tub, then she went back out for two more buckets to heat on the cook stove. When the water was boiling, she poured it in the tub and tested the water; it was fine. She went to the back room and got him a clean towel and laid it on the table with a bar of lye soap.

"Try not to get your wounds wet with your bath-water," said Sue. "We'll come in after you wash and get your britches on. I washed up your dirty clothes, so you've got clean ones again. Then I want to look at your dressings to see if they need changing before you put your shirt on."

The ladies went into the bedroom while Card went into the kitchen. He undressed and got in the warm water. It felt so good, but he didn't want to take up a lot of time bathing since the women were having to stay in the bedroom.

He bathed, got out, and dried off. While getting dressed he happened to see his reflection in the mirror. He had facial hair and looked kind of scruffy. So, he went to his bag to retrieve his pa's straight razor and shaving mug. He lathered up his face and was shaving when the women came back into the kitchen.

Jean took the razor from his hand and said, "Card, you're in no shape to be handling sharp objects. Now sit down and let me shave you."

He did as he was told and when she was finished, she took a warm rag and washed the remaining shaving cream off his face. He looked in the mirror and nodded his approval as she combed his hair.

Sue examined his dressings and then cleaned up the kitchen. Card went to the living room while Jean took a bucket and emptied the washtub before taking it back outside. He felt so much better after cleaning up and putting on fresh clothes.

CHAPTER SIXTEEN

Card sat thinking about how much time he'd lost since getting shot. Yet he was grateful he'd met the Marshall family, especially Jean. That thought made him smile.

Jean walked into the room as he was smiling with a faraway look in his eyes. She put her hands on her hips. "Excuse me, but what's so funny, Mr. Jordan?"

Card jerked his head around toward her and smiled again. "I was thinking about how pretty you are."

She was the one blushing now. "Is that what you say to all the girls you meet?"

"No, only the really pretty ones."

"Tell me the truth, now…have you ever had a sweetheart?"

"Not yet, but I'm thinking about getting one," said Card, now smiling from ear to ear.

Jean sat down and they began to talk about

nothing in particular. They simply enjoyed each other's company and sat together for a long while. Card wanted to kiss her but thought that might be a little too forward.

Jacob returned from town loaded down with the requested supplies and pulled the wagon close to the front door. Sue, Jean, and Card came out to get the bags of stuff he'd brought back from town. They took it all into the house while Jacob unhitched the horses and stowed the wagon.

Card was waiting for him when he came into the house.

"Mr. Marshall, did you happen to see the man I told you about?" asked Card.

Nodding his head, Jacob said, "Yeah, while I was in the store, him and another man came in. The other fellow was a scrawny, mean looking little man and he was smoking a cigarette. He bought some tobacky, but they only had one bag left and the fellow seemed upset with George for not having more. The man in black took the scrawny fellow by the arm and told him to settle down. Then he asked George when he'd have more tobacky. George told him tomorrow or the next day. He thanked George and they left. I watched them head off toward the saloon."

Card had a hardened expression on his face, and he clenched his fists at his sides.

Jacob looked at Card. "Son, what's this all about? Those are some mean looking men you're wanting to know about."

"Yeah, they are," replied Card, and went to the living room to sit down.

Card sat thinking as he waited for Sue and Jacob to put the supplies up in the kitchen. The good thing was, the gang was still at Honey Grove and he hoped they would stay there a few more days until he was well enough go after them again.

Getting up and walking into the kitchen, he asked everyone to come into the living room and have a seat. He knew it wasn't going to be easy, but he had to tell them what had happened to his family.

"My name is Card Jordan. We've got a small ranch over in southwest Red River County, about four miles northwest of a small settlement called Possum Trot. A little over a week ago, I went hunting for deer when I saw five men riding hard and going south on my first day out. The man in black I asked Mr. Marshall to watch out for is their leader. While I was hunting, they went to my house and murdered my mama, Pa, sisters Mattie and Shelia, and my brother Ben. My neighbors and I and buried my family, then I packed up my supplies and started on the murderers' trail. Before my mama died outside lying on the ground, she wrote in the dirt, 'Card kill them all.'"

Jean had her hands in front of her face. "Oh Card, that is terrible, your entire family is dead." Sniffling, Card said, "Yeah, and that's why I wanted to know if Mr. Marshall saw the man wearing black at town."

"He is there for sure, I seen him in the store today," said Jacob.

Jean moved closer to Card and took his hand in hers. "I'm so sorry that you have to be the one to inflict revenge on their killers."

"I made a promise to my family that I'd hunt every

one of those murdering scum down and kill them," said Card. "I killed one of them over at Paris before I came here. It was in self-defense; he went for his gun and I shot him. I was cleared of any wrongdoing by Marshal Dover and Sheriff Gose in Paris. There's wanted posters on all the members of the gang, and the posters say dead or alive. I'm not a cold-blooded killer, I made sure he drew first."

Sue pointed her finger at Card. "Now you listen to me, young man."

Jacob reached over and put her hand down. "Sue, it's time for you to listen."

Sue closed her mouth and stayed silent.

"Card, none of us ever thought you would kill anyone in cold blood," said Jacob.

Card pulled his hand free from Jean's grip. "I'm sure the man wearing black is the one that tried to kill me on the trail the other day. He was at the saloon when I shot the other man. I can't ever repay the hospitality you folks have shown me, and you have been good friends. I was really sick when I came here. You took me in and nursed me back to health and if it's okay, I'd like to stay until I am fully well. I don't think I can do what I need to do in the shape I'm in right now."

Jacob leaned closed to Card. "Son, you're welcome here as long as it takes to get you well, none of us wants you going out doing what you've got to do if you're not well enough to carry out your promise."

"I appreciate you letting me stay and I'll pay you for your trouble and such," replied Card.

"Are you fast with that six-shooter?" Jean asked, pointing to his gun, which was lying on top of his bag.

"Yes, I am. I'm very fast and I hit what I shoot at."

"Good, because I have invested too much time taking care of you for you to get yourself killed," Jean said.

Jacob and Sue laughed. Jean was embarrassed and hid her face in her hands.

"Miss Jean, I surely don't intend to get shot and I plan on coming back by here when I'm done," said Card, while taking hold of her hand. "Especially now, just to see your pretty face."

They all had a good laugh.

They had a big meal that night. Card liked sitting and talking with the Marshall family, even though it wasn't his own. The more he got to know them, the better he liked them all. Especially Jean.

After they had eaten, Sue said, "Card must be on the mend the way he ate tonight, since he pert' near ate two plates full."

"If the food wasn't so good, I wouldn't eat so much," said Card smiling.

Card had a restless sleep again with dreams. He dreamed about his family being alive and all of them having fun, then suddenly the scene changed and he saw them all lying dead.

He awoke to a dark room, frightened. He stayed awake until first light, then got up and sat in a chair thinking about what he was going to do when he found Ned Black. Ned and his men were the reason he was alone without family and had already killed one man. He shook his head and thought, *two weeks ago I had never even thought about killing someone and now I've killed one man. And I plan to kill four more.*

Sue and Jean came from their bedrooms and went into the kitchen and started breakfast while Jacob went to the barn and gave some grain to Smoke and the other animals. When Jacob came into the house, everyone sat at the table and ate.

After breakfast Card and Jacob went to the barn and Card found a curry comb and brushed his horse's back and neck. Smoke stood still and let Card brush him. Card went through his supplies and made sure he still had a coffee pot and skillet. He unrolled his bedroll to let it air out since it had been rained on.

He was tired by the time he finished caring for Smoke and looking at his things, so he walked back to the house and sat down in a chair and closed his eyes and went to sleep.

Sue and Jean went about their daily chores and let him rest until it was midmorning.

Card woke up and went into the kitchen. Jean had fixed some sandwiches and poured some water in a fruit jar.

"Well sleepyhead, did you decide to get up?" asked Jean.

Card pointed to the sandwiches. "What are you doing with the food and water jugs?"

She touched his cheek. "Card, it's a beautiful day outside. Put your coat on and we'll go for a walk and have a picnic."

"Oh good, that sounds like fun," said Card as he

went to the living room and put on his coat and hat. Then he walked into the kitchen to find Jean holding a food basket. He reached for the basket, but she pulled it away and smiled. "You just tag along on this trip and maybe next time I'll let you carry everything."

"Yes ma'am," said Card. "I'll surely let you lead the way," as they went out the door laughing.

Card had a delightful time walking with Jean. It was a beautiful day, just like Jean had said it was.

They found a place where they could sit down and eat the food, she had prepared for them. He was feeling much better by the time they got back home.

Card recuperated at the Marshall's farm for the next twelve days. By then his headaches were gone and some of the soreness in his shoulder had left. He'd spent the time helping around the barn fixing things and feeding the livestock. He would chop wood to strengthen his arm and shoulder. When he didn't have chores to do, he would go out behind the barn and practice drawing his gun.

Jean made sure they took a walk every day and usually brought food for a picnic.

They showed their affection for each other by holding hands and giving each other kisses.

Card was feeling much better both physically and emotionally because of his time with Jean.

He still had dreams about his family, but he was learning how to cope with them, even though he had to keep reminding himself they were just dreams.

On the night of the tenth day with the Marshalls, Card realized his stay at their farm was close to being over. He decided that after a few more days of healing, it would be time for him to leave and continue the mission he had started.

The next morning after breakfast, Card told them his news. "I really hate to say this," he said as his eyes watered up, "but it's time I complete what I have to do. If It's okay with you, Mr. Marshall, I'll spend the day here and get all my things ready but in the morning, I've got to ride on."

Jean didn't even let her grandpa get a word in before she expressed her disappointment. "No, please don't go! I want you to stay here with us," she said, touching his arm lightly.

"I made a promise to my dead family to avenge their murders," said Card. "The longer I stay here, the less I want to fulfill that promise. If I don't do this now, I may never have the opportunity to see it through."

Jean began to sob but she raised her head and said, "Card, you know I care for you and I'm so proud of you for wanting to keep your promise to your family. Now I want a promise from you that when this is all over with, you come back to see me."

Jean got up and walked behind his chair, leaned over, and put her hands on Card's shoulders. She kissed him on the cheek.

Card looked at Sue and Jacob with a happy expression on his face, although his cheeks were a little flushed.

Jacob blew on his coffee before taking a sip and looked at Card. "Son, when a man makes a commitment, he has to make difficult decisions. I wish you would stay here longer but I understand you have to follow through with the promise to your family."

Sue got up and went to Jean and hugged her neck, then she walked over to Card and hugged him. "You can stay here as long as you want. We all love you like a family member."

"Thanks, I love all you guys also," said Card while wiping his eyes with the back of his hand.

Card and Jean spent the entire afternoon together. They took a walk and found a good place to sit in the tall grass under an oak tree and shared their feelings about life and each other. It was a passionate time, kissing and touching each other as they expressed their love.

The next morning after breakfast, Card and Jacob went to the barn and saddled Smoke.

"Mr. Marshall," said Card, "I would like to leave my pack horse here, if that's all right with you. I'll give you some money to pay for your time and feed."

Jacob removed a lead rope off a peg. "You can leave the horse here and I'll take care of it."

Card handed him some money. "Take this money, and I really appreciate you."

"Thanks, Card," said Jacob. "I appreciate your generosity."

Card loaded his provision sack and his clothes bag. He rolled up his bedroll and decided to take it and the tarp, which he tied on the back of his saddle. When he was finished loading his provisions, he led Smoke to the front door of the house.

Sue and Jean came out to say goodbye. He hugged Sue, then hugged Jean. She stood on her tiptoes and kissed him square on the lips. His face turned red, and she smiled and giggled.

Card mounted Smoke and headed toward Honey Grove. He hoped that Ned and his men were still there. But even if they had moved on, he'd still find them and kill them.

CHAPTER SEVENTEEN

I t was bright and sunny, which made the day feel more like late August rather than late November. Card rode at a good pace, loping and walking Smoke the ten miles to Honey Grove.

He wanted to get Jean out of his thoughts and focus on Ned and his gang, but he failed miserably. It was hard not to think about her and the kiss she had given him when he'd left.

He heard a loud, thunderous explosion off to the south. "What the heck was that noise?" The blasts brought him out of his remembrance of Jean. He looked toward the south and saw huge clouds of dust rise into the sky. He had no idea what the explosions could have been from, but he hoped it wasn't something bad.

As he neared town, he saw a sign with an arrow pointing to the south with the words *William Floyd & Sons Quarry* painted on it in big bold letters. So that was what all the explosions were—they were mining stone.

Card didn't want to draw attention to himself as he walked his horse down Main Street in Honey Grove, so he kept his hat down low and slowed Smoke's pace as he checked out the town. The post office was centrally located, and he could watch both ways down the street from there. He tied his horse to the hitch rail in front of the saddle shop and walked to the post office, where there were some benches on the side-walk. He sat down and observed the town and enjoyed the fine weather.

Across the street was the Smith Hotel. It looked like it had been here for a while because the paint was faded and there were a few warped boards on the front wall and the windows had not been cleaned in a long time. There was dust and cobwebs on them…on one side of the hotel, sat a dress shop, and on the other side was a shoe cobbler.

Card sat for over two hours and watched folks going about their daily chores. Some people were shopping and others were working at the different businesses. He liked trying to figure out what kind of work someone did by their appearance and mannerisms.

He saw two men cross toward the west side of the street about two blocks north of where he sat in front of the post office. He continued to observe them as they walked in the direction of the mercantile store, or maybe they were headed to the gunsmith shop which was next door to the north. He was about a block away from them at his location at the post office, but he remembered that directly across the street from the mercantile store was the marshal's office.

That little scrawny fellow is the one they call Smokey, and the other one is Bill.

Card watched as they went into the store.

He got up from the bench, checked his gun to make sure it was loose in the holster. His hands were shaking, and he was beginning to sweat. He thought about his family lying dead outside the house, then took some deep breaths to calm his nerves. He walked west across the street while watching the men go into the mercantile. He stayed on the sidewalk until he stopped between the store and the newspaper office. He didn't want to make his play inside, since there were innocent shoppers inside. He would wait until the men came out before approaching them.

He tried to wait patiently but it was difficult. His heart was pounding.

Smokey came out and leaned his back against the front porch post, pulled out the makings for a cigarette, and started rolling. He put the finished cigarette in his mouth and lit it with a wooden match.

Card took a deep breath to calm his nerves. He looked at his hand to see if it was still shaking. He closed his eyes and said a short prayer, asking forgiveness for taking another life.

Let's get this show started, thought Card as he stepped out from between the two buildings and onto the sidewalk and took about six steps toward Smokey, then stopped. Smokey turned his head toward Card, looking startled.

Card rubbed his fingers and thumb together on his

gun hand. "Smokey," he said slowly. "You are a murdering thief. You killed my family and stole my pa's horse, and now it's time to pay your dues and die."

Smokey smiled calmly. With his left hand, he removed the cigarette from his lips and flicked it at Card's face while at the same time going for his gun with his right hand.

Card had been watching Smokey's eyes and was waiting on him to try something. Suddenly his instincts took over and he drew with lightning speed, shooting Smokey straight through the heart. Smokey never cleared leather before he tumbled backward from the impact of the .44 lead. He slammed onto the sidewalk, dead.

Card hurriedly walked into the store looking for Bill.

"Mister, that other fellow done run out the back door!" the store clerk said through trembling lips. "Scared to death, I reckon."

The deputy marshal ran into the store with his gun drawn.

Card stopped, raised his hands and said, "Deputy, my name is Card Jordan. There's a wanted poster on that man out there in the marshal's office. I'm not a bounty hunter, but he's part of a gang that killed my family and I shot him in self-defense. He drew first and the other one called Bill left through the back door a few seconds ago."

The deputy looked around the store. "Did any of you see what happened?" he asked.

Card pointed to a woman holding her hand over

her mouth. "Deputy, she saw it all through the window."

The deputy took her statement and instructed her to come to the marshal's office later and sign a written statement.

"Mister," said the deputy. "Do you know his name?"

"Yeah," replied Card. "He is Smokey Thomas and he rides with Ned Black and his gang."

"I have heard of Ned and his gang," said the deputy. "We were notified they may be in the area a few weeks ago. We never thought they would come here."

The deputy looked at the store clerk. "Send someone to notify the undertaker about the body," he said.

"Okay, I'll send my boy after him," said the clerk.

Next, he searched through Smokey's pockets and collected his valuables. He pulled out a few things and stood up to talk to Card. "Follow me to the marshal's office and we'll discuss this with him."

They walked across the street and into the office, where the marshal raised his head up from a stack of paperwork. "My name is Marshal Finnis Thomas, and I don't like shootings in my town. What exactly happened, son?"

Card explained the whole story to the marshal about his family getting murdered, the bank robbery, the killing of Big Bob, and now how he'd just killed Smokey.

"Did you notify the undertaker and search the dead man?" Marshal Thomas asked the deputy. "If this boy's story is right, he should have had money on him."

The deputy laid all Smokey's valuables on the desk.

Marshal Thomas pointed to a chair. "Card, you sit down while we look through my wanted posters."

He rifled through them and then looked up at Card. "It's your lucky day," he said. "There's a poster on that man. It says there's a $10,000 reward on him and you are also entitled to his valuables."

"Marshal, that money was stolen from the bank in Reno and needs to be returned. You can sell the rest of his stuff and apply whatever it brings to pay for his burial, and if there's any left over, you can have it," said Card.

"I'll notify the authorities in Reno about the money when I get time," said the marshal. "I've been really busy lately, but I get to it in a day or two."

"Thanks, Marshal," said Card. "I'm sure the fine people in Reno will appreciate it."

"If you keep looking, you'll also find posters on his so-called friends," said Card. "You can have the reward money wired to my bank back home. If you will give me a pen and paper, I'll write down all the information."

"Yeah, you do that, and I'll get it taken care of as soon as I can," said the marshal.

Card wrote it down and handed the paper to the marshal. "Marshal Thomas, am I free to go? I've got work to do."

After looking the paper over, the marshal nodded.

"Yep, you're free to go and don't come back to my town causing any more trouble."

Card went to his horse and mounted up. He rode through town to see if he could see any signs of the other members of Ned's gang.

He stopped at the livery stable and asked, "Did a man dressed in black clothing accompanied by two other men leave here today?"

"Yeah, those boys lit out of here about an hour ago, right after that shooting at the store," said the stableman. "I reckon they were in a big hurry, because they left their supplies in one of the stalls. I guess they're mine now."

"Do you know which way they were headed when they left town?" Card questioned.

The stable hand pointed west. "I guess they're headed to Bonham, that there is my guess from the direction they took."

"I'm much obliged," said Card, and handed the man a silver dollar.

CHAPTER EIGHTEEN

Ned and TC were gathering up their belongings when Bill came in the room breathing hard. "What's wrong?" Ned asked.

Bill held up his hand, indicating he needed a second to catch his breath.

"That young feller that killed Big Bob caught Smokey outside the store on the sidewalk and gunned him down," said Bill. "It was the darndest thing I ever saw. He said something to Smokey, and Smokey went for his gun. The gunfighter put a bullet in old Smokey before he could even clear leather. I'll tell you the truth he's the fastest I've ever seen."

Ned's surprise caused his mouth to fall open. He was certain that he had killed the fast gun out on the trail. He was mad, the gunman was still alive but also from hearing that from Bill. It upset him something fierce that one of his men would think the young gunman was so fast.

Ned looked at Bill with rage in his eyes and shouted, "Why didn't you try to shoot the kid?"

"I didn't have a shot. I was inside the store when it all happened," Bill said. "I came back here as fast as I could, to warn you that he was in town."

"Did anyone see you come in?"

"No, I left out the back door of the store and ran all the way here by the back way," replied Bill.

TC put his bag on the bed. "Ned, how do you want to handle this?"

Ned thought for a moment. "Grab your things, we're leaving here quick. The law will be looking for us as soon as they figure out who Smokey is. I told you before we got here, the marshal would only turn a blind eye to us as long as we didn't cause him any trouble."

"Yeah, just as well," said TC. "I was getting tired of this place anyway. It's too bad this is going to spoil our plans of robbing the bank."

Ned grabbed his things. "There's another town and another bank, let's get packed up."

Ned, Bill, and TC left town with their horses in a full run, headed west on the main road.

Ned was mad as a wet hen for having to leave town before they could steal more money.

It was time to confront his men and let them know his expectations.

Ned turned off the road and stopped where he could talk to Bill and TC. "All these excuses about why, no one has even tried to kill this gunman, stops today. I have big plans to rob some banks and have some fun. From now on when you see him, each of you had better be putting slugs in that kid."

"I'm sorry that I didn't do more, but after seeing him draw, I know I'm no match for him in a standup fight," said Bill.

"Then I suggest you figure out what you're going to do the next time you see him," said Ned. "Now let's get going."

They rode their horses hard trying to put some distance between them and whoever it was that was after them.

He was also mad that Smokey was dead, and he was frustrated with Bill because he hadn't tried to shoot the man. He was angry that the gunman was still alive after he put two bullets in him.

He had been so sure he'd killed the boy and that had been the end of it. He was mad that he'd been wrong.

Ned slowed his horse and let TC come up beside him.

"What's up, boss?" asked TC.

"The more I think about it," said Ned, "The more it's just reasoned that that boy after us is a bounty hunter."

"Could be," said TC. "He seems to have the skills for it. So, what's your plan now?"

Bill rode up to join the conversation. "Anything I need to know, boss?"

"Yeah," said Ned. "We think that young killer is a bounty hunter and after us for the reward."

"Do you have a plan on how we're going to kill him?" asked Bill.

"I'll let you know when the time's right," said Ned. "Let's keep moving for now."

They'd ridden about seven miles when they started to approach the small town of Windom, Texas.

By this time the horses were hot and lathered up, so Ned told his men to slow to a walk for the last quarter mile.

"This little town is only five years old," said Ned. "There ain't enough money here to even consider robbing. It's known as a flag town because the railroad has a water tank located here where the locomotives can take on water. It's got one church, a small school building, and one general store, along with about twenty houses."

"Well that definitely ain't nothin' worth robbing," agreed Bill.

There were water troughs along the street, so they stopped long enough to let their horse's drink. When they had their fill, the gang walked on through town.

There was a sign with an arrow pointing west: *Bonham 11 miles.* They sped the horses into a lope until they had ridden another four miles and came to Dodd City, Texas. Ned decided to circle around the outskirts of town and try to conceal their tracks. If that bounty hunter was following them, it might confuse him for a little while and slow him down.

They passed by Dodd City and returned to the road. They had been quiet for miles, but finally Bill spoke up and said, "My horse is getting really tired, we need to take a break."

Ned didn't pay any attention to Bill or acknowledge his remark.

When they came to Bois d'Arc creek, Ned said, "We'll walk the horses downstream a way, to cool them down and let them drink. I would suggest if you have anything to eat in your saddlebags, you better get it now. This will be the only time we stop until we get to Bonham."

They came around a bend in the creek and stumbled onto a campsite.

"Hello in the camp!" Ned called out.

They were sitting on their mounts looking around when a voice spoke from behind cover.

"Everybody put your hands on those saddle horns, we got you dead to rights."

Ned and his men did just what the voice said. The man sounded familiar to Ned, but he couldn't quite tell who it belonged to.

"I'm Ned Black," he said. "And I recognize that voice. Who are you?"

Two burly looking men came out from the trees, both were smiling. "Hello Ned, it's been a long time."

Joe and Ed Sloan were old running mates of Ned's. They had ridden together about three years back, when he had first gone out on his own. The brothers were very dangerous men, but could be trusted to pull their weight in any situation.

"Get down and sit awhile! The coffee is hot and strong," said Joe.

Ned, Bill, and TC dismounted obligingly.

Ned told TC, "Take the horses to the creek to get a drink."

TC nodded and led the horses away. Everyone else

got their cups out and found a place to sit around the fire.

Bill pulled a sack of stale jerky out of his saddle-bags and passed it around. They all took some from the sack and tore off chunks of the tough meat.

Ned took a sip of the black coffee and smiled. "Boys, that is some fine coffee."

"Yeah, it is," said Joe. "Ed can't cook worth a hoot, but he can make good coffee."

"What're you men doing in these parts, anyway?" Ned asked. "The last I heard, you were in Mexico."

"We've been in the Rocky Mountains all summer, and are heading back to warmer weather," said Joe. "So, we're just passing through. In fact, we were getting ready to break camp and get back on the road when you showed up."

The brothers went on to explain that they were trying to get clear of Fannin County because they'd killed a man over by Savoy the day before and wanted to put some distance between them and the law.

Ned's cup was almost empty when TC came back with the horses and sat down to drink a cup of coffee and chew on some jerky.

"Smokey and Big Bob are dead," said Ned. "They were gunned down by a bounty hunter. Never even had a chance with him." Then he had an idea. "Boys, we've been over the mountain and across the creek together many of times, and I know how you operate and what you can do. How about I give you three hundred dollars and if you happen to come across the bounty man, you take care of him for me?"

Joe and Ed looked at each other.

"That sounds just fine," said Ed.

"Ned, we're sorry to hear about Big Bob getting gunned down," said Joe. "I never cared much for Smokey, so no love lost."

"I agree with you about Smokey, all he ever did was puff on a cigarette and complain," said TC.

"Big Bob was a good friend and a fine one to ride the river with," said Ned. "He was with me longer than anyone."

"What does this bounty hunter look like?" asked Ed.

Ned looked at Bill. "Bill, tell them what he looks like so they can take care of him for us."

"Well, he's young, and wears an Army Calvary hat. And he's tall, I'm guessing about six feet three, and had on a brown shirt and vest the last time I saw him," said Bill. "Oh yeah, he rides a dapple-gray horse."

The brothers nodded thoughtfully and Joe said, "We'll be glad to help out. He's as good as dead."

Both of the brothers laughed, and Ned smiled.

Ned got up and motioned his men to follow him over by the horses, out of hearing range.

He whispered, "Each one of you give me a hundred dollars for your share for them killing the gun hand."

Ned gathered the cash from his men and took the money over to the brothers.

"Joe, you and Ed be careful if you see this feller," Ned said. "I sure do appreciate you taking care of him for me. Maybe the next time we meet up I can buy you a drink."

"Ah Ned, we know you'd do the same for us," said Ed. "The fact is, we enjoy killing bounty hunters."

"We need to get back on the trail," said Ned. "We've got an appointment in Bonham later today."

Ned and his men got back on the road. It wasn't far to Bonham, so they took their time and didn't push their horses. Ned was happy knowing the brothers would kill the gunman for him.

Now I can get on with my business without looking over my back.

CHAPTER NINETEEN

C ard was standing with his back to the street while his horse drank from the water trough. He could see across the street from the reflection off the window in front of him.

He saw two men come out of the saloon and it alarmed him when they looked his way while they talked. He watched them take their coats off and reach down to take the safety thongs off their guns.

Card removed the safety thong from his gun as the men started across the street and walked up behind him.

He became cold inside, and he felt his heart rate increase as his instincts took over. When the two men reached the middle of the street, Card turned around real slow, with his hand by his gun, rubbing his fingers and thumb together, ready for action.

The brothers were startled when he turned toward them ready to draw.

"You fellows are about to make a big mistake," said Card.

"No sir," Joe said, and spit tobacco juice on the ground. "You made the mistake when you started following our friend, Ned Black. Now it's time for you to die."

Card's face went cold. "You're scum just like he is. Are you going to stand there talking or pull those hog legs and pay your dues and meet your maker today?"

Both brothers went for their guns.

With lightning speed, Card pulled his gun and started firing. Joe was hit first; his gun fell to the ground as two .44 slugs penetrated the left side of his rib cage, shattering his heart.

Ed was at least able to clear leather before he was hit in the chest twice. He fired one bullet into the ground and then fell face first into the dirt.

Both brothers were dead.

Card stood in the street and ejected the spent shells from his gun and reloaded. Then he holstered his weapon and waited, because he knew the town's lawman would want to talk to him.

Sure enough, the marshal came running toward the bodies. He kneeled to check if the men were dead.

"Did you kill these men?" he asked as he got to his feet.

"Yes, sir, I did," Card said. "They came after me and I defended myself."

"I'm Marshal Snead," said the man. "These here hombres are Joe and Ed Sloan. I've got wanted posters on them. Sheriff Lipscomb over in Bonham sent me a telegram today to be on the lookout for these two scoundrels. He's after them for murdering a fellow just down the road from the Savoy Male and Female College."

"My name is Card Jordan from southwest Red River County. I believe the brothers were put up to killing me."

About that time the undertaker came to see if he might have some new business. He seemed happy to discover he did.

Marshal Snead searched the dead men's pockets and found $630.

"Follow me to my office, and we'll take care of some paperwork."

They got to the jail, and Marshal Snead found the wanted posters on the brothers. The men were wanted dead or alive, each with a $500 reward.

"Marshal," said Card. "I'm on the trail of Ned Black and his murdering gang. They killed my family and stole our horses. They also robbed the bank in Reno."

"Yeah, I remember seeing a telegram about that a few weeks ago," said Marshal Snead.

"There's wanted posters on Ned and each of his men," said Card. "Marshal, those brothers told me when they made their play that they were friends of Ned's. They were going to kill me for Ned, that's why they came after me."

"I'll send Sheriff Lipscomb a telegram letting him know you killed the Sloan brothers," Marshal Snead said. "You wouldn't by any chance be headed to Bonham, would you?"

"Yeah, I'm going there next. But I would like to stay here in town long enough to get something to eat, being that it's getting late. That is, if you don't mind," replied Card.

"That's fine. In fact, I think I'll join you," said Marshall Snead.

"Sure," said Card. "But first give me a pencil and paper and I'll write down where you can have the reward money sent to."

"When you're finished, you can start on over to the chow hall," said Marshal Snead. "I'll stop off at the telegraph office and send a couple of telegrams, then meet you there. Go ahead and order me whatever you are going to have, I'm not particular on what I eat."

Card smiled at the remark. "Yes sir, I'll get your food ordered."

He went out the door and led his horse down the street to the café, where he tied Smoke to the hitch rail. He loosened the girth strap and rubbed his horse's neck, telling him he would be back soon.

Card opened the door and walked into the diner. There were tables placed evenly around the room. Some had chairs, and some had long wooden benches. All the tables had bare wood tops with no tablecloths.

Only a few people were sitting at various tables eating their supper. When he started toward a table where he could face the door and street, people began to whisper to their dining companions.

Card smiled and walked to his table. He overheard an old man say to a younger man, "Boy, that's the fastest draw I've ever seen. I swear, I believe if he squared off with John Wesley Harden, he'd win."

Card sat there, wondering who John Wesley Harden was. He'd never heard of him before. But whoever the man was, he must be fast with a gun.

The waitress came over. "Hello, stranger. We have fried chicken, fried taters, beans, and cornbread on the menu today."

"That sounds good," said Card. "Oh, and bring Marshal Snead a plate also, he's on his way over. I'll have coffee to drink, but I don't know what he will want, so you can wait on his drink."

She smiled and walked to the counter, pulled down two cups and filled them with coffee and came back to the table. She put them down and asked Card, "Are you new in town or passing through?"

"I'm passing through," said Card. "I'll eat and be on my way."

"I'll have the food out in a couple of minutes."

"Thanks, ma'am," said Card, smiling as the girl turned away.

Marshal Snead came into the café. He greeted the town folk and walked to Card's table, where he sat down and took a drink of coffee. "I notified Sheriff Lipscomb in Bonham about the Sloan brothers being killed," he said.

"I hope it's a relief to the sheriff to know those brothers won't be causing him any more grief," said Card.

Marshal Snead handed Card his bank information. "I won't need this anymore. I went ahead and sent the information to pay the rewards on the Sloan brothers to your bank."

"Thanks, Marshal, I appreciate it," Card said.

Card looked up as the girl came out with two plates heaping with food. He hadn't noticed earlier how pretty she was. She had black hair and a great smile.

She set Marshal Snead's plate down first, and then moved around the table. She set Card's plate down and placed her hand on his back. "If there is anything you need, just let me know, my name is Ruth." Marshal Snead grinned at that.

Card smiled and tore into his food like he hadn't eaten in a week.

Marshal Snead took a few more bites, then he looked at Card. "I do believe Ruth has a crush on you," he said, smacking on his food.

Not looking up, Card said, "Maybe, but I have a girlfriend back toward Paris."

The marshal laughed. "I think Ruth will be sad to hear that."

Card shrugged and kept eating.

When his food had been devoured and he'd sopped up the last of his gravy with the remaining cornbread, Card finished off his coffee and pulled four dollars out of his pocket. He put it on the table.

"I appreciate all your help, Marshal," said Card. "This should cover our meals."

"Thanks for the food, and I hope you get those men you're looking for," said Marshal Snead.

"I need to get back on the trail. It'll be after dark when I get to Bonham."

Marshal Snead stood up, stuck out his hand and said, "Card, good luck on finding those men."

Card shook his hand. "Marshal, maybe I'll stop back in when all this is over."

When Card was outside, he mounted Smoke, turned toward Bonham, and started out of town at a lope. After he had traveled about two hours, he saw lights on the horizon.

CHAPTER TWENTY

Ned and his men stopped at the east side of Bonham, Texas. "Find you a room over at the saloon," he told Bill and TC. "I'm going to stay at the Bonham House Hotel. We don't want to cause any trouble or have anyone suspect anything."

"What do you want us to do?" Bill asked.

"Well, I'm gonna scope out the town," said Ned. "I want the two of you to stay put at the saloon until I develop a plan."

"I like that idea," said TC. "I'm ready for something to drink, and a woman."

"I'm going to put my horse up behind the hotel in their stable. You boys find a place to put yours up tonight, and tomorrow you can have them boarded at the livery stable if we decide to stay longer."

Before Ned checked in at the Bonham House Hotel, he removed his gun belt and put it in his saddlebags. He didn't want anyone to recognize the distinctive gun, or him because of it. He carried his saddlebags into the hotel and told the clerk he needed a room and a hot bath.

The clerk pushed the register book across the counter for Ned to sign. "That'll be six dollars for the room and hot bath," said the clerk. "You'll be in room nine, that's on the bottom floor down the hallway. Your bath will be ready shortly."

"Much obliged," said Ned.

As Ned went to his room, he made a quick observation of the hotel lobby. Then he walked down the hall all the way to the back door and opened it and looked outside. Once he was satisfied, he had figured out an escape route, he went to his room.

He lay on the bed to rest for a few minutes, giving them time to get his bath ready. He waited for what he guessed to be close to thirty minutes before taking his shaving mug, straight razor, and gun with him to the bathroom. He got into the tub of hot water, reflecting on his situation. The whole trip seemed to be going wrong. Two of his men were dead and the rest of them were running like scared kids.

Bill had had a chance to shoot but had run instead. Maybe he couldn't depend on Bill anymore. He hoped the Sloan brothers had been able to kill that gunman. If not, he'd have to do it himself.

After his bath, Ned didn't feel like going to the saloon to drink. He decided to go into the hotel dining room and have his supper instead.

CHAPTER TWENTY-ONE

onham was alive with coal oil lights placed along the sidewalks, and some businesses were still open after dark. Card figured it must have been about seven o'clock. He wanted to get a lay of the town before he began to search for Ned and his gang.

He rode down Main Street and saw the livery stable, stagecoach station, and a building with a sign that read *Drake's Mercantile*. Bonham seemed like a good-sized town with lots of businesses.

He rode until he came to the town square. In the middle of the square was the courthouse and jail. One particular business that got Card's attention was Russell's Opera House. Signs out front of the opera house were advertising a performance of *Uncle Tom's Cabin*.

Card thought fondly of his mama. She would've loved to see that play; she was always having him and his brother and sisters read about plays and such.

Card went around to the sheriff's office, hoping to meet Sheriff Lipscomb in person.

He introduced himself to the deputy on duty and asked after the sheriff.

"He's gone home for the night but will be back early tomorrow," the deputy told him.

"I'll be back tomorrow and visit with him," said Card.

"I'm Deputy Lewis. I'll tell the sheriff you came by, if I see him before you get back."

"Thanks, it's nice to meet you Deputy Lewis," Card said.

Card decided to look over the rest of Main Street before he began to look for Ned. He saw another livery stable close to the west edge of town. He stopped, dismounted, and walked inside to find the stable hand mucking stalls.

"I'm looking for three men that came to town this afternoon, and was wondering if you've seen them," said Card. "One of them dresses in black and wears a fancy gun."

The livery stable hand shook his head and said, "No sir, I ain't seen nary one that meets that description, and we don't have any new horses in the stalls today."

"Okay, thanks," Card said. He walked to where Smoke was, mounted up, and turned back the way he had come.

As he neared the square again, he saw a man wearing a shiny metal star on his vest. Card guided Smoke over to the lawman.

"Pardon me sir, would you happen to be Sheriff Lipscomb?" asked Card.

The man looked up and said, "Yep, I'm Sheriff Smith Lipscomb. What can I do for you?"

"I'm Card Jordan and I'm the man that killed the Sloan brothers. I'm on the trail of Ned Black and his gang. They murdered my family and robbed the bank at Reno, Texas."

"Do you think they're in Bonham?" Sheriff Lipscomb asked.

"I'm not for sure yet, but just so you know, there are wanted posters on each member of his gang."

"Young man, what are your intentions if you find them?" asked Sheriff Lipscomb.

"Sheriff, I made a promise to my mama, Pa, sisters and brother that I'd kill those men and that's what I intend to do," replied Card.

The sheriff nodded his head. "I figured as much. Just be careful and watch your back. Those old boys are all mean and wouldn't think twice about shooting you in an ambush."

Card touched the brim of his hat before saying, "Thanks, Sheriff. Maybe I'll see you tomorrow. You have a good night."

"Good night, young man," said the sheriff. "It was nice meeting you."

Card turned and rode on down the street.

He stopped at the first livery stable he had seen when he came into town and found the stable hand and questioned him. "Did three men riding together come by here today? One of them is dressed in black clothes and wears a fancy pearl-handled gun."

"No, don't reckon I saw anyone like that today," he said.

"Much obliged," said Card. He walked away then turned back to ask, "Is there some other place in town where they could board their horses besides the livery stables?"

The stable hand thought for a few seconds and said, "There's a stable out back of the saloon, but it's fairly run down. I reckon someone could use it, though. There's also another one out back of the Bonham House Hotel, for hotel guests only."

"Thanks," said Card. He mounted and decided he would ride around the backs of the saloon and hotel with the hope he could find the horses belonging to Ned and his men.

There was a side street close to the hotel that took him to an alley behind the buildings.

He stopped when he got to the hotel stable, dismounted, and looked inside. It had only one horse in it so he figured they must not be in the hotel.

Next, he walked Smoke to the saloon stable. This old stable was in bad shape, and it was empty.

Card wondered if maybe he had second-guessed himself about them stopping in Bonham. As he turned to ride back around to the livery stable to board Smoke for the night, he heard a horse nicker from behind the old stable. It had come from a grove of trees.

Card tied Smoke up to an old corral post. He pulled his gun from the holster and walked slowly, listening for any sounds. As he got closer to the trees, he could hear horses chomping on the winter grass. He continued until he walked up against some ropes that were being used for a makeshift fence. He eased around the horses, gun in hand, making sure no one was standing guard. When he was satisfied that he was alone, he stood in the shadows and thought the situation out. He reasoned that at least two of them were in town. Why else would someone hide their horses here instead of taking them to the livery?

The first place he would look was the saloons. Ned must've gone on past town, or he was hiding out somewhere else and not with the other two.

Card walked where he'd left Smoke, mounted, and rode back to the livery stable.

"Howdy," said Card. "I would like for you to feed my horse some oats and rub him down."

"Yes sir," said the boy as Card handed him two dollars. He decided to leave his coat with his saddle since it was a mild night, and he didn't need anything to get in his way in case there was trouble.

Card walked across the street and onto the side-walk and made his way to the saloon where he stood out front looking in the window. He took in the appearance of everyone inside but didn't see Ned or his men anywhere. Maybe they were in another saloon. Just then, a couple of men walked away from where they had been standing at the bar. Now Card had a clear view of what he'd been looking for.

TC stood in front of the barkeep having a drink. Card knew it was him from the description on the wanted poster and from his memory of that day on the trail, the very first time he'd seen him on the way home from hunting.

Card kept looking but didn't see Ned or the man named Bill.

He was positive it was TC when he pulled a watch

out of his shirt pocket and checked the time. That was all Card needed. It was his pa's watch that TC was looking at. TC was alone, so it was time for Card to make his play.

Card reached down and removed the safety loop off his gun, then looked at his hand to see if it was shaking. His hand was steady.

I've come a long way since I left home. I'm not even scared and shaking this time.

He took one step toward the door and paused. He closed his eyes and prayed that his mama and pa would give him strength, speed, and calm for what came next.

Then Card stepped through the batwing doors in one smooth, fluid motion and stood to one side to let his eyes adjust to the dim, smoke-filled room. The piano player was pounding out an off-key tune. Some men were playing poker, while others drank and talked to the saloon girls.

He walked toward the bar and stopped about six feet behind TC. The man looked up and their graze met in the mirror behind the bar. TC sat his glass down and turned around slowly.

"Mister, I don't know you, and I don't like anyone coming up behind me, not even people I do know. So, you better say a quick prayer 'cause I'm going to kill you right here and now," said TC. "But before I do, tell me who you are and why are you trailing us."

Patrons in the saloon started moving to get out of the line of fire.

Card said confidently, "My name is Card Jordan. You and your murdering friends killed my family over in Red River County a little over five weeks ago and now it's time to pay your dues and die."

TC sneered. "I remember that! I'm the one that killed your ma. I shot her out in the yard."

TC began to move his left hand real slow up to his shirt pocket. Card knew he was trying to distract him, so he just kept looking at TC's eyes and rubbing the fingers and thumb of his gun hand together.

TC pulled out Card's pa's pocket watch and pushed the button to open it, at the same time he went for his gun.

TC was faster than most men...but not this last time.

Card's hand was ablaze with speed and he shot with deadly accuracy.

TC managed to clear leather just as a .44. slug entered his skull right between his eyes causing blood and brain matter to spray onto the mirror and bottles of liquor behind the bar.

The saloon smelled of gunpowder and smoke filled the area. Card opened the chamber on his gun, expelled the spent cartridge, and loaded a new one before putting the weapon back in his holster. He bent down and grabbed TC's left hand. A great sense of relief filled him as he pried the man's fingers open and took his pa's pocket watch from the dead man's grip.

"Send someone for Deputy Lewis," Card told the barkeep.

CHAPTER TWENTY-TWO

B ill walked into the dining room where Ned sat eating his supper. When he saw Ned, he made his way to the table and leaned over and whispered in Ned's ear, "TC is dead. He was gunned down by that bounty hunter."

Ned was overcome with anger and sat staring at his plate, his hands in fists under the table.

"Bill, go out back and saddle my horse," he said. "He's in the hotel stable. I'll be there directly, and we'll talk."

Bill tried to interrupt, but Ned gave him a wave of his hand and said, "Go, now!"

Ned couldn't believe it. He was sure the Sloan brothers had been able to kill the gunman. Bill was useless, and now he had to leave again because of Bill's cowardice.

Ned finished eating his supper and thought about what he'd do next. Then he went to his room and put on his pearl-handled gun and gathered up all his things.

Bill had just finished getting Ned's horse saddled when Ned came out of the hotel wearing his gun belt and carrying his saddlebags and rifle. He put the saddlebags on behind the saddle and tied them in place with the saddle strings.

"Ned, my horse is back behind the saloon in the trees," said Bill.

"Shut up, Bill. Tell me exactly how TC was killed, and don't leave anything out." He had fury in his eyes and he spewed spit as he talked.

"Well," said Bill. "You see, I was setting over by the wall talking to two of the saloon girls. My back was to the crowd, so I didn't see the bounty hunter come in the door. TC was at the bar drinking. I heard a commotion and saw men moving around. I got up just in time to see that bounty hunter draw and shoot TC. TC didn't have a prayer against him. He got shot between the eyes. Ned, I swear that kid is fast, he's real fast! I didn't have an opportunity to do anything except sneak out the back door and come straight to warn you."

Ned looked at Bill with a bloodthirsty rage in his eyes.

"You coward, you've had two opportunities to kill whoever that gunman is, and not once have you done anything but stick your tail between your legs and run like a scared sissy," growled Ned. "The running stops here and now. You're not riding out of here with me as long as that fellow is alive."

Bill started to reply but Ned grabbed him by the

front of his shirt and pulled him closer until they were eye-to-eye.

"Bill, I want you to kill him, and I don't care how you do it. If you don't kill him, I'll kill you, do you understand?"

Bill shook his head. "Yes. Yes."

Ned turned him loose and said with a stiff face, "I'm heading to Colbert's Ferry and then back to Indian Territory to hole up at my cave in the Kiamichi Mountains. If you kill him, you can come find me, but I better not ever catch sight of you if you run away again."

Bill was visibly shaken by Ned's demeanor. He said, "Ned, I'll kill him and come find you."

Ned mounted up and left.

CHAPTER TWENTY-THREE

Card was still standing at the bar when Deputy Lewis came into the saloon. The deputy kneeled and checked to make sure TC was dead, then got up and looked at Card. He shook his head and said, "It looks like you found one of those outlaws. What's this fellow's name?"

"He's TC Stewart and he drew first, so I shot him in self-defense," said Card.

Deputy Lewis looked around the room and asked, "Did any of you fine men see what happened?"

A few men who had seen the shooting told the deputy that TC drew first, but he was no match for that man over there. They all pointed at Card.

The undertaker came and looked the corpse over before asking for help to get the body over to the funeral parlor. The deputy told him to wait a minute so he could search the dead man's pockets. He took everything, including the gun. Then he told the under-taker he could take the body.

The barkeep was cleaning the blood and brains off the mirror and bottles, as if he did it every day.

Deputy Lewis told Card, "Follow me to the sheriff's office. We'll need to do some paperwork."

He turned to a man who was standing nearby. "Go get the sheriff and have him come to his office," he said.

The man nodded and left to do as he was told.

When they got to the office, the deputy asked Card, "Do you want a cup of coffee? I just made a fresh pot."

"Sure." Card took a cup and sat down.

Sheriff Lipscomb came into the office as Card finished his coffee. The man didn't seem to be in a good mood from being disturbed so late at night. He said, "So, young fellow, you come into my town and start shooting it up?"

Card sat in silence while the sheriff got a cup of coffee.

Finally, he spoke. "Sheriff, I told you what I was going to do with that murdering scum," he said. "He drew first, and I shot him in self-defense. However, I could've walked in there and shot him in the back and still be in agreement with the law. He's wanted dead or alive, according to the wanted poster you've got over there." He pointed to a wall full of posters.

Sheriff Lipscomb smiled and said, "You do have some sand in you. I'll give you that, and I don't blame you for doing what you did. I just wish it had happened somewhere else, that's all."

"I understand, and will try not to shoot anyone else in town tonight," replied Card.

The sheriff laughed. "Well, let's hope you don't have to. One shooting is enough."

"Do you want the reward money sent to the same place as the money for the Sloan brothers?" asked Sheriff Lipscomb.

"Yes, if it's not too much trouble."

The sheriff turned to his deputy. "Did that outlaw have any money or valuables on his person when you searched him?"

The deputy handed the sheriff the money he had taken from TC's pockets. "This is all he had on him, Sheriff," said Deputy Lewis.

"That money was stolen from the bank in Reno, Texas," said Card. "I think you should get it back to those people."

"I'll make sure the money is returned to the bank," said Sheriff Lipscomb. "What're your plans now?"

Card thought for a second. He looked at the sheriff and said, "I think since it's so late I'll get a room at the hotel and sleep on a good soft bed tonight. In the morning, I'll start back hunting the last two men and kill them."

"I think that's a good idea about sleeping in a soft bed. I do believe I'll go back home and get in mine," said Sheriff Lipscomb. "You have a good night, and maybe I'll see you tomorrow."

"Thanks, Sheriff," said Card. He got up, shook hands with Sheriff Lipscomb and Deputy Lewis then walked out the door and headed to the hotel to rent a room and take a hot bath.

CHAPTER TWENTY-FOUR

C ard walked across the street on his way to the hotel when he heard the sound of a single rifle shot and took notice of a bullet wheezing past his head. It sounded like it had been a close one. He dropped to the ground and rolled as another bullet hit the dirt near his leg and stirred up dust.

He pulled his gun as he continued rolling and tried to look up the street for another muzzle flash. If there was another shot, he would shoot to both sides of the flicker of rifle fire and hope to hit the shooter.

Sheriff Lipscomb and his deputy came running out of the jail with guns drawn. They saw Card on the ground.

"Are you hit?" the sheriff called out to Card.

"No, I'm fine. Just dirty." Card got to his feet and dusted off his clothes. He could still feel a little soreness in his shoulder from his healing bullet wound.

Sheriff Lipscomb saw the grimace on Card's face

and asked, "Are you sure you're okay? You look like you're in pain."

"I'm fine," said Card. "I fell on my shoulder is all."

Card watched Deputy Lewis go back inside the sheriff's office and return with a lantern. He walked up the street toward where the sound of the shooting had come from. He stopped at the intersection of Main Street and a side street, and on the ground was two spent .30-.30 cartridges. He picked them up, put them in his pocket, and continued to search the ground, most likely for footprints, Card guessed.

Deputy Lewis walked back to Card and the sheriff. "I found where the shooter rode out of that side street and fired two shots with a .30-.30," he reported. "Then he must've turned and headed back the way he came really fast, from the way it look like his horse was tearing up the ground. I would suspect he is finished for the night."

Sheriff Lipscomb shrugged and said, "Nothing more can be done tonight so you may as well go on to the hotel and get cleaned up."

"Thanks, Sheriff," said Card. "I appreciate you." He picked his hat up off the ground and continued on to the hotel.

He walked into the lobby and up to the counter, where he hit the bell with the palm of his hand. The clerk came from down the hallway with a cup of coffee in his hand.

"May I help you, sir?" he asked.

"I'd like a room and a hot bath," said Card.

"That'll be four dollars for the room and two dollars for the bath," replied the clerk.

Card nodded and counted out the money.

"We'll wash your dirty clothes for an additional dollar," the clerk added.

"Okay," said Card. He handed seven dollars to the clerk.

The man counted out the money and gave Card the key to room number six.

"The bath will be across the hall in room number five, and it'll be ready within thirty minutes."

"Thanks," replied Card.

Card went to his room, pulled off his boots, and looked in his bag for his straight razor. He figured he might as well cut off his facial hair if he was going to take a bath. He gave himself a decent shave in his room, then put his gear back in his bag. As an afterthought he also put his gun in the bag, just in case someone decided to disturb him while he took his bath. He grabbed his bag and walked across the hall to room five.

When he opened the door, a woman was pouring hot water in a large bathtub. She looked up, smiled and said, "You can come on in, I just finished. There's a clean towel on the table. I'll wait in the hall for you to get undressed and in the water. If you'll put your dirty clothes by the door and holler, I'll wash them and hang them up to dry."

"Thank you, ma'am, I appreciate it," said Card. "I'll be leaving early in the morning and was hoping I could get them back early."

"I'll hang them in the kitchen where it's warm," she said and closed the door on her way out.

Card took his gun out of the bag and laid it on the

table so it was within reach. He removed his clothes and put them by the door and got in the tub. He called out to the woman and let her know he was decent. She opened the door, gathered up his clothes, and told him she would bring them to his room first thing in the morning.

Card took some lye soap, lathered up his hair, and sank down in the water to wash the soap out. After he had scrubbed the dirt and grime off his body, he sat back and thought over the last few days.

Ned had orchestrated three attempts on his life—so far. By all rights, he should be dead. But he knew he had his guardian angels watching over him. Thank you, family.

As he replayed the events of the day, he realized that he had stopped shaking when he got ready to draw, or even feeling scared, like he had at first. He didn't even feel sad or have any remorse for killing those five men. His entire young life he'd been taught to love others as you would yourself, but the Good Book also said—in some passage he couldn't remember—an eye for an eye and a tooth for a tooth. Those men were murderers that were getting their justice, served by him.

He wondered how Jean and her family were doing. She sure was pretty. And that kiss she gave him when he'd left the Marshall's ranch sure did feel good.

He shook his head, spraying water across the room. He couldn't be thinking those kinds of thoughts until he finished what he had to do.

Card got out of the bathtub when the water got cold. He dried off and found another pair of long johns in his bag, so he put them on. He took hold of his bag in one hand and his gun in the other and eased the door open. He looked both ways down the hall to make sure no one saw him in his long johns, then hurried into his room.

It was time to turn in. Someone had already tried to shoot him once tonight, so he took the chair and propped it against the door. Card climbed into bed, placed his gun close by on the nightstand, and looked up at the ceiling.

Mama, I killed the worthless piece of horse dung that shot you today. Rest easy, I love you.

Tears filled his eyes once again. He pushed those thoughts away and instead went over each one of the shootings in detail. He realized for the first time that he rubbed his fingers together right before he drew his gun.

Daylight was streaming through the cracks in the curtains when he woke up the next morning. He was snuggled in the warm bed thinking how good it felt compared to the ground, when he heard a knock on his door. He eased out of bed with gun in hand and stood beside the door. He opened it a crack to see the hotel woman standing there with his clothes, so he told her to set them on the floor and he'd get them when she left. He watched her walk away before opening the door wide enough to get his clothes.

He dressed, combed his hair, buckled on his holster and gun, put his hat on, and grabbed his bag. In the lobby, the hotel clerk said that breakfast was in the dining room if he had a mind to eat before his journey.

"Much obliged," said Card.

He went into the dining room and sat down. The same lady that had washed his clothes came over with a cup and a pot of hot coffee. She set them on the table and asked what he would like for breakfast. Card told her he would like a plate of biscuits and gravy, and some bacon. She nodded her head and went to the kitchen.

Sheriff Lipscomb came into the dining room. He saw Card and walked over to his table and took a seat.

"Morning, Card, mind if I sit down?"

"No sir, I like your company."

"I did a little checking this morning and that feller in black lit out of town last night at a dead run, traveling north. I suspect he is heading to Savoy or maybe Sherman. And I'm pretty sure he left right after you killed old TC. The fellow that took those potshots at you last night was in the saloon when you killed TC. He was over on the other side of the room talking to a couple of the working girls when that ruckus started. He turned tail and ran when he saw you kill TC."

Card picked up the coffee pot and refilled his cup. "So, the one they call Bill had his back to me. I was wondering where he was last night. I'll have to be more careful in the future and not make that mistake again," said Card as he took a sip of hot coffee.

Sheriff Lipscomb removed his hat and ran his fingers through his hair. "I'm almost positive he's the one that tried to kill you last night. I would say he's probably holed up somewhere on the road to Savoy, waiting to bushwhack you along the trail."

"Sheriff, I thought it was Ned that took those shots at me last night since he's tried it before. Based on this new information it seems like he's put a death warrant out on me," said Card.

"Yep, I'm thinking Ned ordered Bill to gun you down any way he can."

"I'm figuring on that also," agreed Card. "And when I finish my breakfast and have one more cup of coffee, I'll load up and ride north. I'll take extra precautions and be looking for any place where a man could lay in wait for an ambush."

"Now that you've got my two cents, I'll be moseying along," the sheriff said.

"Have a cup with me, I'm in no big hurry to leave," said Card. "I'll let the back-shooting polecat wait in the cold for a while."

Sheriff Lipscomb laughed and said, "Son, I was right—you do have sand in your blood. Okay, I'll have one cup with you."

Card motioned for the woman to bring another cup to the table. She poured it full of coffee and set it down in front of the sheriff, who took a sip of the hot, black liquid.

"But a word of advice from an old veteran lawman," said the sheriff. "When this is over, let it be over. You go back home and pick up the pieces of your life and carve out your own place in history, raising cattle or such."

Card took a big swallow and set his cup down. "I appreciate it, Sheriff, and that is my intention," said Card. "I met a pretty young filly back over between Dodd City and Paris that I'll probably go see on my way home when all this is over. But for now, I've got a job to do that don't concern her."

They both finished drinking their coffee. Card stood up and stuck out his hand and the sheriff shook it. He motioned for the woman to come back over, and he gave her five dollars and thanked her for his bath, clean clothes, and food.

Her eyes went wide with surprise at the generous tip. "Thank you, sir! You come back any time, you hear?"

Card nodded his head.

Card and Sheriff Lipscomb walked out onto the sidewalk, where the sheriff started to his office, and Card went to the livery stable.

CHAPTER TWENTY-FIVE

C ard left Bonham and headed north toward Savoy, Texas. He decided to go slow and be extra careful because he had a feeling that Bill would try to kill him soon. Card rode along and scanned the countryside looking for anything that seemed out of place. Every so often he would stop his horse, take out his looking glass, and watch for a potential threat along the edges of the road. He watched for birds taking flight or animals running off as he continued down the road. After riding an hour, he noticed a sharp curve in the road about a half mile ahead. He stopped and took out his looking glass to get a better view. Suddenly Smoke's ears pricked up. Whatever it was that had alerted Smoke caused Card to feel uneasy. The sharp bend in the road was a likely place for someone to hide. He sat for a moment to gather himself. His instincts or guardian angels were warning him of danger.

With a flick of the reins Smoke turned back the way

they had come. This would get him out of sight from anyone who might be hiding at the curve in the road. After about five hundred feet, he turned toward the west. Then he rode a wide swath to the west until he came to a gully. It looked like the gully went in the general direction of the road. Not wanting to make any noise, he was careful not to brush up against any trees or bushes as he guided Smoke down into the ravine and walked him toward the road. Smoke warned him again by swiveling his ears forward. It was time to dismount and tie his horse in a spot where he could graze on the dead grass. From there, Card crept along the bottom of the gully until he saw a horse tied to a bush.

He approached the horse carefully, not wanting to spook him or cause him to nicker. He rubbed the horse's head behind his ears and neck before he continued down the pass. He could see where someone had climbed out, by the way the ground was torn up. Not knowing where the person was located, Card climbed up the bank a few yards farther south. Hopefully he could keep the element of surprise when he found whoever was up there.

The climb to the top of the gully bank was slow and he stayed on his stomach as he looked around. His eyes caught the faintest hint of movement to his left, over by a log. Using extreme caution, he eased closer. When he was close enough without being heard, he concealed himself behind a tree and used it for support and a shield as he began to stand. Now with his presence obscured, he could watch the man behind the fallen log. He was pretty sure it was Bill Hill, but he needed to be certain.

The man rose his head up to look over the log and Card saw his face and recognize him as Bill.

It's time, Card stepped out from behind the tree while getting in position to draw. Unmindfully he began to rub his thumb and index finger together.

"Bill Hill, you murdering piece of trash, you killed my family and now it's time to pay your dues, so get up and face me like a man."

"Now hold on a minute," said Bill. "I'm going to get up real slow, so don't shoot." He began to stand up. He pushed himself up to one knee, took hold of a tree for leverage then leaped to his feet, bringing his rifle up to shoot.

But Card was waiting for his trick. His hand flew to his gun and with lightning speed he fired one time, hitting Bill in the stomach.

Bill dropped his rifle and clutched his left side as he fell to the ground. He was sobbing and moaning in pain as Card walked up and kicked his rifle away. Card reached down and pulled Bill's handgun out of its holster and threw it into the brush.

He looked down at Bill's wound, and it seemed like the bullet had gone in more to the side of his torso, rather than straight into his stomach.

"Bill, get your handkerchief and hold it to the wound to stop the bleeding," said Card.

Bill cried out in pain as he removed his handkerchief from his pocket and applied it to the wound.

Card grabbed Bill by the arm. "Roll over so I can see if the bullet went all the way through."

Card pulled Bill's shirt up and saw where the bullet had gone through and left a mangled-looking exit hole. He took his own handkerchief and covered the wound with it. It was apparent he'd have to do more so he grabbed Bill by the shoulder and turned him back over while the man cried out in pain.

"I'll help you on one condition. Tell me where Ned is heading," said Card. "He left you all alone to die out here. He deserted you and doesn't care if you live or die. Now you can lay here in agony and die alone and let the buzzards peck your eyes out and eat your flesh off the bone, or I can patch you up as best I can and take you back to Bonham to the doctor, it's your choice."

Bill moaned. "All right," he said with a faint voice. "I'll tell you, but you've got to promise to take me back to town for help."

"Start talking," said Card.

"I didn't want to shoot at you, but Ned made me. He said he'd kill me if I didn't kill you," Bill said. "Ned is turning southwest at Savoy and going to Colbert's Ferry on the Red River. He's got a place in Indian Territory in the Kiamichi Mountains. It's a cave where someone built a shack at the entrance, years ago. That's where he's heading to spend the winter."

"I need better directions than that, since there's a lot of territory to cover in those mountains," said Card.

"Okay, just give me a minute. I'm hurtin' some-thing terrible," said Bill. He took a few short breaths before continuing. "About forty miles or so north of the Red River is a tiny settlement by a spring. It's called Kuniotubbee. It's in the Choctaw Territory called Pushmataha. The best I remember, you go west from the spring about a mile or so, turn north, and ride until you come to the Kiamichi River."

Bill stopped talking and tried to take in deeper breaths of air.

"Get on with it. The faster you tell me what I want, the faster I'll get you to the doctor."

"Okay, okay. When you come to a sharp bend in the river, turn northwest and continue until you come to a small creek. Cross it and ride until you come to Buck Creek. It's a fairly large creek with some deep holes in it. Ride north up Buck Creek until you come where it runs into Wildhorse Creek. That's where you'll have to look closely. You'll see a large rock, and behind it you'll find the trail up to his hideout."

Card was satisfied with the directions and said, "Bill, lay still while I go after the horses."

Card picked up Bill's rifle and took it with him. He brought the horses back and told Bill to mount up or he'd throw him over the saddle and tie him on his horse.

Bill had lost a lot of blood and was too weak to pull himself up to mount his horse. Card grabbed him from behind and lifted him up into the saddle. Bill cried out from pain, but Card didn't care since Bill was murdering scum and didn't deserve to be treated kindly.

With lengths of pigging string, Card tied Bill's hands to the saddle horn and his feet into the stirrups. Then he mounted and leaned over to take hold of Bill's horse's reins and started back toward Bonham. Bill kept moaning and complaining about his pain, but Card kept on riding and not caring.

Bill was losing more blood as they rode, and he lost consciousness about two miles from town. Card led Bill's horse straight to Dr. Pinwell's office. When they got there, Card dismounted and checked on Bill; he was dead.

Good riddance, another murderer dead.

Card went into the doctor's office. "I've got someone outside on his horse. I'm pretty sure he's already dead, but you can check on him if you want."

Dr. Pinwell grabbed his stethoscope and went outside where Bill was leaned over on his horse. The doctor listened for a heartbeat, shook his head, and told Card, "He's dead all right."

Thanks for checking," said Card. "How much do I owe you, Doctor?"

"One dollar will do," said Dr. Pinwell.

Card paid the doctor, mounted his horse, and rode to the sheriff's office with Bill in tow.

The sheriff walked out of his office and down the steps onto the street as Card pulled up. He watched as Card tied his horse to the hitch rail.

Sheriff Lipscomb walked over to Bill and took a good look at his face. "Deputy Lewis!" he hollered. "Come outside, I need some help."

They took Bill off his horse and laid him on the sidewalk.

Sheriff Lipscomb told Deputy Lewis, "Go get the undertaker."

"Okay, Sheriff," said the deputy. "It seems like he's getting a lot of business lately."

Then the sheriff searched through Bill's pockets. He found a roll of money, a pocketknife, and a .41 caliber derringer.

"Sheriff, I'll take that hideaway gun if you don't mind," said Card. "You can dispose of the rest of his belongings."

"I'll send a wire to have the reward money sent to your bank," said the sheriff.

"Much obliged," said Card.

The undertaker came and collected Bill for burial and when he left, Card went inside with Sheriff Lipscomb and Deputy Lewis.

He told them what Bill had told him about Ned heading into Indian Territory.

"Card, there's some rough country north of the Red River and some rough people," said Sheriff Lipscomb. "You can ride back to Paris and turn north to the Red River. I believe you'll ride through Goodland and then on up to the springs where some Indian families live. If you go that way you can probably save yourself three days of riding."

"I think I'll take your advice and go that-way, Sheriff," said Card. "Ned won't be expecting me to get there ahead of him."

Card stood up and shook hands with Sheriff Lipscomb and Deputy Lewis. "I'm much obliged for all your help, maybe I'll see you fellows again sometime."

"I would like that," said the sheriff. "You be careful in those mountains."

"It's been my pleasure to meet you, Card," said Deputy Lewis as he patted Card on the back.

Card walked out to his horse and headed for Paris.

CHAPTER TWENTY-SIX

It was about noon when Card left Bonham. He figured if he rode hard, he could make it to the Marshall's farm before it was too late in the night. Hopefully they'd still be up.

Card stopped in Dodd City only long enough to water Smoke and grab a sandwich from the café. He ate in the saddle so he wouldn't waste any valuable time. He kept pushing on; he was on a mission. Jean was on his mind, and he couldn't think about anything else. He thought about what he would do when he saw her.

I'll hug her and kiss her on the mouth so she'll know how much I missed her. Yep, that's what I'll do.

He slowed Smoke down as he rode into Honey Grove. He wanted to let his horse cool down before drinking his fill from the water trough. It was a short water stop before moving on to the Marshall's farm.

Card was tired and hungry when he saw the lights of the Marshall's homestead. He stopped a little way from the house to holler out and alert them they had company. Jacob Marshall opened the door and asked, "Who's out there?"

"It's Card Jordan, Mr. Marshall. Can I ride on in?"

Suddenly the door flew open and out came Jean, running to meet him. He hurriedly dismounted, held his arms out to her and Jean fell into them, kissing him square on the lips. He was a little surprised but also proud as a peacock.

Sue came outside and stood beside Jacob. She said, "You two lovebirds might as well come in the house before you catch your death out here in the cold."

Card and Jean held hands as they walked into the house. Everyone sat down and Card said, "I'm really glad to see you all. It seems like ages since I left here."

Sue was the first to speak up. "Did you kill those men yet?"

Card told them a little about what had happened and why he had stopped back by.

"I'm on my way to Indian Territory to find Ned," said Card. "After Ned's dead, then I will have fulfilled my obligation to my family by avenging their deaths."

"Card Jordan, when was the last time you ate anything?" Jean asked, changing the subject abruptly.

"I had a sandwich on the road over by Dodd City," replied Card.

She stood up. "You get yourself up and follow me into the kitchen," she ordered.

When they were in the kitchen she turned around and whispered, "No man of mine is going to go hungry." She stood on her tiptoes and kissed his lips again. He wrapped his arms around her and pulled her close, basking in her kisses and when he turned her loose, she giggled and started rustling up something for him to eat.

Card sat at the table admiring her beauty as she hurriedly warmed him up some food. He could still taste the flavor of her lips; they tasted like cinnamon.

Jean set his food on the table and told him to eat up.

Card dug into a big bowl of vegetable soup and tore up chunks of cornbread to drop into the hearty liquid. He was in hog heaven. A beautiful girl and delicious hot food, what more could he ask for?

He finished his soup and Jean came back to the table with a piece of apple pie.

"Card, I baked this pie all by myself," said Jean.

He took a big bite and said, "This is the best pie I've ever eaten."

"You, silly man," she said, and leaned over to kiss his face. Card loved every minute of it.

"Card, I wish you wouldn't go into Indian Territory to follow that man. They say there's a lot of dangerous people hiding out from the law there. I was hoping you'd stay here with us."

"Jean, I'd love to stay here, but you know I've got a responsibility to fulfill the promise I made to my family and if I don't follow through it'll haunt me for the rest of my life. I hope you know that I love you and want to be with you, but I need to finish what I started."

She came over to him and sat down in his lap and put her arms around his neck. She looked him in his eyes and said, "Card Jordan, I love you too. I understand you've got to finish what you started but I just want to be with you."

He kissed her and said, "We need to go back to the living room. I need to talk to your grandparents about something important."

"Let's go," said Jean. She took Card's hand and led him to the other room.

"Jacob, What's the best way for me to get to the Red River north of Paris?" Card asked as he sat down. "I need to find a small community in Indian Territory called Kuniotubbee. There's supposed to be a spring close by where some Indian families live. I'll be going up in the mountains north of there to find Ned and kill him."

Jacob set thinking a moment. "When you leave the farm, head northeast for about four miles and you'll intersect with a road running east and west. Turn east and that'll take you to a little town by the name of Lenior. At Lenior continue northeast until you find a road running north and south."

Card nodded as he tried to memorize the directions Jacob was giving him.

"That road will take you to the Red River," continued Jacob. "It's the main road between Indian Territory and Paris. Then you can ride north from there to a settlement where there's a store and such, called Goodland. It's a Presbyterian orphanage and school for Indian kids, and you can buy any supplies you'll need at the store. Continue on north about another twenty miles to the settlement by the spring."

"Thanks, Jacob," said Card. "Do you know about how long it will take me to get there?"

Jacob rubbed his chin. "From here, I'm guessing the better part of two days."

"Will I be in the mountains soon after I cross the river?" asked Card.

"No, you won't get to the mountains until you're north of that spring community," said Jacob, shaking his head.

Card sat silent for few seconds before talking. "I've got to finish the promise I made to my family, but when it is all over, I'd like to come back here and ask you for permission to marry Jean. That is, if she is willing to have me as her husband."

Jean began to cry with joy. "Yes, yes, yes!" she said through her tears.

Card reached over and took her hand in his.

Jacob looked at his wife and then back to Card. "Son, we'd be honored to have you marry our grand-daughter. But for now, you need to be very careful and come back in one piece from your trip to Indian Territory."

Jacob stood up, reached his hand out to Sue and said, "Honey, let's turn in and leave these young'uns to talk some before it's their bedtime. Card, you can use the spare bedroom tonight and we'll see you all in the morning for breakfast."

"Good night," said Card.

"Good night, Grandma and Grandpa," said Jean.

As soon as Sue and Jacob left the room, Card grabbed Jean and kissed her with such passion that she let out a sigh and melted into his arms. When he broke the kiss, he looked into her eyes. They were sparkling with happiness.

"When I get back," he said, "I'll spend a few days with you. Then I'll need to get the rest of my horses at Paris and take them to my ranch. I've got things to do before you get there. It'll be a little rough for a while, but we'll manage just fine. I've got enough money to buy more land and cattle so I can provide the very best for us."

"I don't care about any of that. All I want is to be with you for the rest of my life," replied Jean.

"It's important to me that I provide you with safety and security," said Card. "I've got an idea for a new business, but I'm not ready to discuss it yet."

"Well, when you're ready to talk about it, I'll listen. But I'm going to love on my big handsome cowboy right now," said Jean as she snuggled up to Card. He smiled and turned a little red but loved her playful mood.

The night passed quickly as they sat flirting with each other, as two people do when they are in love, holding hands, laughing, and talking about their future together.

It was getting late when Card said, "Honey, we need to go to bed."

Card took Jean in his arms and kissed her. He whispered in her ear, "Goodnight, I love you."

"Good night, darling, I love you more," Jean responded. She went into her room and closed the door.

Card woke up to someone kissing his face and lips, and his eyes came open to see his love leaning over him.

"This is the best wakeup I've ever had."

"You better get used to it, Card Jordan, because I plan on waking you a lot from now on. Now get up, breakfast will be ready soon and I don't like for the food to get cold," said Jean.

Memories of his mama came to him with those words. That was something she had always said. "Yes, ma'am," he said, smiling.

He waited until Jean left the room before he got out of bed and put his clothes and boots on. He looked at himself in the mirror and combed his hair so he was presentable, and went to the kitchen where there was a hot cup of coffee waiting on him.

Jacob was already seated and having his first cup of coffee. Sue was finishing up cooking while Jean was setting the table and laying out some of the food. When everyone was seated, they held hands and Jacob blessed their food. Sue passed the bowls around the table. There was bacon, eggs, fried taters, cathead biscuits, and gravy. There was butter and even some plum preserves that Sue and Jean had canned back in the summer.

They ate in silence and when everyone was finished, Card said, "If you don't mind, I'd like to spend another day here. One more day's rest will do me and Smoke a lot of good. I need to go through my supplies and clean my guns."

Jean smiled from ear to ear.

"I think that's a good idea. Another day won't hurt one iota," said Jacob.

"I can help you clean your guns, Card," said Jean. "I clean Grandpa's for him."

"I'd like that. And maybe we can wash my dirty clothes," said Card.

"Jean, let's get this table cleaned off and the dishes washed before you start being a gunsmith," said Sue.

Jean made a sad face but gathered the plates and bowls off the table and put the leftovers away.

Card and Jacob got their coats on and walked to the barn to feed the livestock.

Card fed Smoke a helping of oats and rubbed his neck. He picked up each of the horse's hooves and inspected the shoes to make sure none of them were loose or wore down. He looked at the underside of his saddle and examined the leather for cracks in case he needed to clean it with saddle soap.

He needed something to do to pass the time, so he went through his grub bag and decided he had almost enough provisions to get him to Indian Territory but wanted to get some more jerky.

Maybe he would ask Sue later if she could spare some. That along with what he already had would do fine until he stopped at the store at Goodland.

Card took his rifle back to the house with him so he could clean and oil his weapons. Jean was waiting on him in the kitchen. When they finished with Card's guns he told Jean, "I'm going out back and chop wood, so Jacob don't have to."

Card went to the backyard and picked up the axe. He split kindling for the kitchen stove. He loaded up an armful of the tinder and took it in the kitchen and filled up the box where it was kept. Then he went back outside and started cutting firewood for the fireplace and the kitchen stove.

He was strong, and his shoulder was almost totally healed. He could swing an axe with the best of them and when he was done, he had over a rick of wood. Jean came outside to help. As he split the logs, she stacked them. They worked together for about three hours before Jean told Card, "It's about dinnertime. I'll go in the house and fix us something to eat. We can eat out here if you want to."

"That'll be great. I miss our picnics," said Card.

Jean grabbed him around the neck and kissed him. "Don't go anywhere, I'll be right back."

"I won't go anywhere, woman. I never leave when there's food coming."

She went into the house shaking her head and laughing.

She prepared sandwiches of ham and leftover taters, and she brought them outside where Card was still working. He put down the axe and drew a bucket of water from the well to wash his hands.

Card sat down beside Jean and she handed him a sandwich. He took a big bite and looked at her. "This is my first ham and fried tater sandwich, it's really good," he confessed.

She smiled and started eating hers.

When Card was almost done, he looked up and saw a big buck deer feeding under a tree out in the pasture.

"Be real still," he told Jean. "I'm going after my rifle."

Card moved slowly to the house, walking through it and out the front door, and then ran to the barn. He grabbed his rifle from his gear and ran back the way he had come. The deer was still there, so he leaned the gun against a tree limb and took careful aim and squeezed the trigger. The deer fell dead where it stood.

Card leaned the gun against the tree and started out across the pasture toward the fallen buck. When he got to it, he took his knife and slit its throat to bleed it out, then rolled up his shirtsleeves and proceeded to cut its stomach open to remove the guts.

Card hollered to Jean, "Tell Jacob to bring a horse down here to haul the deer."

Jean hurried to the house.

Card finished field dressing the deer and they picked it up and loaded it across the back of the pack-horse. Jacob took it to the shed where they hoisted it up using a rope over the rafter so they could skin it.

Sue and Jean came out and brought a pan of water and some cloths to clean and wrap the meat in. Card skinned the deer, then began cutting off the shoulders and Jacob quartered it up. Sue and Jean cleaned off any remaining blood before wrapping it in the cloth.

Sue told Jacob, "Keep the backstrap out and we'll have it for supper tonight."

"Oh good," said Jacob. "Chicken fried back strap is my favorite."

They made quick work of dressing out the deer and carried all the meat except the backstrap to the smokehouse for storage.

When they were finished with the deer and Card had washed up, he asked Jean, "Will you trim my hair up a bit since it may be a while before I get another haircut?"

"I sure can. Go get your straight razor and comb

while I get the scissors," she said. "I'll meet you out back."

He went to his room, grabbed his bag, and headed to the backyard. Jean had a chair, towel, and some hot water waiting. He gave her his razor and comb, and she went to work like a professional barber, repositioning his head as she went. She put shaving cream on his neck and his face and gave him a shave.

Card was a little apprehensive at first when she used the straight razor on him, and he winced as she began on his neck.

"I shave Grandpa all the time, Card. You have nothing to worry about, and besides I've shaved you before without cutting your throat."

"Yes, you have, I forgot about that," said Card.

When she was satisfied with how it looked, she soaked the towel in hot water and washed off his head, neck, and face.

He gathered up his things while Jean gathered up hers, and they went back into the house.

Card looked at himself in the mirror. The reflection he saw was not the same one he remembered from a month ago. He stood and stared. His looks were maturing. His mind and spirit were not those of a sixteen-year-old deer hunter anymore. Now he was a grown man, hunting other men instead of deer. He scowled at his reflection, surprised that he could have transformed so much in such a short time.

I guess that's what happens when disaster dictates your future for you.

He shook his head and walked to his room to put away his bag.

CHAPTER TWENTY-SEVEN

Card and Jacob sat in the living room talking about cows, horses, and farming until they both got sleepy.

They were asleep in their chairs when Jean came in to call them for supper.

After blessing the food, they began to fill their plates and Jean reminded everyone she'd baked a pie for dessert.

Card took a drink of water. "That's mighty nice of you. I'm sure we'll all want a slice."

"I know I will," said Jacob.

Everyone ate and talked about the day's events, but no one brought up the fact that tomorrow Card would leave again to pursue Ned Black and kill him.

After supper Card and Jacob were sitting in the living room talking again when Jean came in and sat down beside Card on the couch.

Sue came into the room next, carrying a bottle of whiskey and four glasses. She set the glasses down and poured the whiskey. She gave a glass to each of them, then lifted hers up for a toast and said, "Here's to Card and Jean."

They drank their whiskey. After swallowing hard, Card and Jean coughed and shook their heads and grimaced from the taste.

"Whiskey tastes a lot better with honey and sugar in it," said Card.

They all laughed.

"Yes!" exclaimed Jean. "That burned all the way down to my toes."

"It'll get your attention, all right," said Sue.

The room was silent for a moment, until Card changed the subject. "While we're all together here, I have a question that I've been wanting to ask. Why is Jean living here with you?"

Sue started to speak, but Jean interrupted her. "My parents and me used to live in Fort Worth," she explained. "Daddy owned a freight wagon and hauled freight between Dallas and Fort Worth. One day Mama went with him on a haul like she did a lot of times. I was nine years old and stayed home by myself. On their way back from Dallas, the authorities think some men tried to rob them. They think Daddy was trying to outrun 'em when a wheel broke off the axle and the wagon turned over and killed them. After the funerals I came to live with Grandma and Grandpa."

"Did they ever catch the men that tried to rob them?" asked Card.

Jean shook her head and Card could swear he saw tears in her eyes.

"I'm really sorry you had to go through that," he said. "You and I both know what it means to lose our parents."

He reached over and took Jean's hand in his.

"I want to tell you all something. I started out on this journey a scared boy, not knowing what I'd do when I found those men. I didn't know if I could pull the trigger or not. I didn't know if I'd be able to live with myself if I took a life. I've thought about what's happened since I left home. I have killed men, bad men. And to tell you the truth, it hasn't bothered me one bit. I shot them all in self-defense. They were looking me in the eye as I did it. I don't apologize for what I've done or what I'm going to do when I leave here tomorrow. I'll be gone for a while, but I'll be back, you can count on that."

Jean scooted closer to him and hugged his neck. "Card, we love you so much."

"Sonny," said Sue. "We all know the kind of man you have become, and those men got what was coming to them."

"Does Ned know you're following him to his hide-out?" asked Jacob.

"I doubt it, but he's a careful man and he don't take unnecessary chances," said Card. "I'll have the element of surprise on my side, though, since he won't watch for me so soon. I know it'll be a struggle to find him, and I expect him to try to bushwhack me again. It was Ned that shot me the first time, right before I came here for help."

"What'll you do when you find him?" asked Sue.

"I'll confront him," said Card. "I'll tell him who I am and why I'm going to kill him."

Card sat looking at the floor for a moment, and then said, "I'm not a murderer. I'll let Ned draw first, and I'll shoot him in self-defense."

"Son, we know you are not a cold-blooded killer," said Jacob. "You're doing something I wouldn't be capable of doing, and I respect you for making that promise to your family."

Sue put down her whiskey glass. "The question has always been, how do you feel about what you're doing? If you're at ease in your own mind and spirit, then so am I."

Jean squeezed his hand. "Card, you're doing an honorable thing seeking revenge against the murderers that have killed your family. There are probably other families out there that they have hurt. I know you'd never shoot anyone without them drawing first."

Card gripped Jean's hand tightly, never wanting to let go. "I wanted you all to know how I felt and know what kind of man I want to be," he said. "My pa taught me how to fight and how to use a gun. He instilled in me the rule to never start trouble. But he also taught me you don't back away when it comes to you. I'm confident in my abilities and I'll find Ned Black and kill him. Then it'll be finished."

"It's going to be a sad day tomorrow for me when you ride away," said Jean. "But I'm glad this is the last man you've got to go after. Then we can have a lot of time together."

"Yeah, I'll like that," replied Card. "We may even

carve out a piece of history for ourselves along the way."

With that said, they decided it was time to go to bed.

Card said goodnight to Jacob and Sue, and Jean walked with him to his room. They hugged and gave each other a goodnight kiss.

"Card, I'm so proud of you," said Jean. "And I can hardly wait to be your wife."

Card kissed her again. "Dream about me tonight and I'll dream about you."

Jean went to her room and Card closed his door. He undressed and got into bed.

He slept that night without having any bad dreams.

When he awoke the next morning, everyone was still asleep. He got dressed, combed his hair, then went to the kitchen where he put wood in the stove to get the fire built back up. As the stove heated up, he filled the coffee pot with water and dumped in coffee when the water was boiling. It was just about ready when Sue came into the kitchen.

She took two cups and saucers, filled the cups with coffee and placed them on the table. She sat down with Card and poured some of the hot, fragrant liquid into her saucer and blew on it to cool it off a little.

She took a sip and said, "Son, I know what you did and what you're going to do. This ain't something just any man can do. It takes a special person to do all that, and still keep his values and morals in check. Me and Jacob support and pray for you and will continue to until you finish this thing." She reached over and took hold of his hand. "Card, you're a good man and I'm so proud of you."

He teared up and nodded his head in acknowledgment.

Sue started breakfast while Card sat and enjoyed his coffee. Jean and Jacob came in as she finished up. Jacob sat down to a cup of steaming coffee while Jean helped Sue put the food on the table. Everyone was quieter than usual during breakfast. It seemed there was a sadness on everyone's mind, knowing Card would be leaving soon.

"I'll fix you something to eat on the road," Sue told Card.

"Do you have any spare jerky I can take with me?" he asked.

"Yes, I do, you take all you want. I can make more from the deer you shot yesterday."

After breakfast he went to the barn and saddled Smoke and loaded what few provisions he needed. When he was ready, he strapped on his chaps, heavy coat, and gloves, and put on his hat before checking his gun. He led Smoke to the front of the house and left him there while he went inside.

He shook hands with Jacob, hugged Sue, and finally walked over to Jean.

She began to cry and grabbed him around the neck. He held her tight and whispered in her ear. "Jean, you know I've got to go, but I'll be back. This is not good-bye; instead, it's I'll see you in a few days. You've got to be strong for me. I need to know you're strong so I'll be strong. I'll need all my strength and yours to make it through with what I've got to do. I love you and I'll be back."

He kissed her and wiped the tears from her cheeks. He smiled at her and walked out the door.

As he mounted Smoke, Sue came outside and handed him a sack of food. Card touched his heels to Smoke, and they trotted out of the yard heading northeast. He did not look back. It was tougher to leave this time, but Card knew he now had to leave all thought of Jean behind and keep his mind and spirit sharp for what was ahead. Ned Black would not be easy to find and even harder to kill.

Smoke was rested and took to the trail with ease. And with Jacob's directions, Card figured he would get across the Red River easy that first day.

CHAPTER TWENTY-EIGHT

After Ned gave Bill the ultimatum to kill Card, he took the road north that led to Savoy. Ned was in a terrible mood; he knew he should've killed Bill back in Bonham and taken his money. Bill was a coward that couldn't be trusted to carry his weight. If he ever saw Bill again, he wouldn't waste another opportunity to kill him. He couldn't afford to have members of his gang be damn chickens, like Bill.

Ned rode hard the eleven miles to Savoy but slowed his horse down as the town came into view so he wouldn't draw attention and could rest his horse. It had to be around midnight when he finally rode in. He was tired but didn't want to be seen spending the night there.

Water troughs were situated along the street, so he let his horse stop only long enough for it to get a drink. Then he walked his horse through town and increased his pace when they were clear of the buildings.

About four miles west of Savoy, Ned turned his horse off the road and headed in a northwesterly direction toward the Red River. He'd traveled this way before, so he knew where he was going. He had to ride slower since he was going through trees, gullies, and brush thickets in the dark. He could tell by the undergrowth and size of the trees that he must be getting closer to the river bottom.

Getting hit in the face repeatedly by limbs and getting scratched by briars began to make him mad. After another mile he rode down into a gully where he could get out of sight and sleep for a few hours until daylight.

He unsaddled his horse and staked him out to graze. Hunger pains began to hit his stomach because he hadn't eaten since the night before. He looked through his saddlebags and found some stale jerky. It wasn't much but would get him by until he reached Colbert's Ferry and Trading Post tomorrow. Old lady Colbert would probably have some hot food there and maybe something to drink.

Gathering wood was challenging in the dark, but he found enough to build a fire with the hope it would help keep him warm enough. With his bedroll close to the fire, he went to sleep. It was a terrible night sleeping on the ground, hungry, and cold. He was awake when the sun started coming up and was more than ready to get on his way.

As he saddled his horse, he realized he should be getting close to the road that ran from Denison to Colbert's Ferry. He thought he could make it to the ferry at least by late afternoon.

The trail was much easier to navigate in daylight. He stayed away from the brush thickets and rode across cultivated farm and pastureland. There were houses and barns along his path, but he stayed clear of them. About midmorning, he rode up to the road he was looking for and turned north, increasing his speed.

He wanted to get on the other side of the river as soon as possible in case the gunman following him was the law. He would feel much safer after crossing the river, since only a US Marshal could arrest White men in the Indian Territory, and he knew the marshals were shorthanded out of Fort Smith.

The road was a busy one. There were people traveling in wagons and buckboards, on horseback, and some were even on foot. This was the main road between Denison, Texas, and Durant Station, Indian Territory. The MKT Railroad had come through here only two years earlier. The railroad brought with it people, businesses, and the establishment of whole towns along its path.

Ned continued riding hard to cover the six miles to the river.

When he was within view of the ferry, he slowed his horse to a walk. He made sure his gun was ready by removing the safety strap, easing it up out of its holster and then letting it drop back into it again. You never knew who might be lollygagging around a ferry, looking for easy prey. He had taken money and horses off naive travelers himself, close to ferries.

When he pulled up on the south bank of the river, he could see the ferry was on the other side, unloading its passengers. He would have to wait until Old Man Colbert brought it back over.

There was a wagon with a family of Indians stationed close to the loading dock. He walked his horse down to the water and let him drink to pass some time. Then he guided him back up the bank to a good spot from which to observe the area.

Ned dismounted and took a drink from his canteen. He could feel his frustration once again starting to boil to the surface. It was getting old having to wait all the time on someone else, especially when he was in such a hurry. Ned cursed the man silently.

That old fool needs to get back over here.

He had been waiting about ten minutes when he noticed the ferry was coming back across the river. It was about time. He took his horse by the reins and walked down to the loading ramp and cut ahead of the Indian family.

When the ferry pulled up to load, Ned got on first. The family of Indians loaded in behind him. Old man Colbert told Ned, "It'll be two bits for you." He hollered over to the wagon, "It will be four bits for the wagon."

Ned paid his quarter and told Old Man Colbert to get on with the ride across the river, as he was in a hurry. They eased across; the current was mild that day due to no rain the past couple of weeks. The area had a tendency to flood during heavy rains. If the water started to rise, the ferry barge was small enough that three teams of horses could be hitched to it to, drag it up the bank out of harm's way. Fortunately, the trading post was about a mile up the road, and was far enough away that the high water wouldn't affect it.

Once docked, Ned was the first one off, and he made his way directly to the trading post, tied his horse, and went inside.

Mrs. Colbert was minding the store.

"You got any food cooked?" he asked her.

"Ned, you've been here many times," she said. "You know darn well I always have something."

He laughed and smiled at her. "What do you have today?"

"I've got red beans with ham hocks and corn-bread," she replied. "And some hot coffee or home-made chalk, if you're of a mind to drink something."

"That sounds mighty good to me, and maybe a little something special to go in that coffee if you have any."

A few minutes later, she brought him a plate of food and a cup of coffee laced with whiskey.

When she put it all on the little table she said, "Here you go, Ned, and don't let that coffee scald your tongue."

He was hungry but waited long enough before eating to give her a list of supplies he needed.

As she gathered together the items on his list, Ned devoured his food and thought about having another cup of that coffee, but decided he needed to get back on the trail. He still had a long way to travel.

"How much do I owe you for all my things?" asked Ned, reaching into his pocket for some of his cash.

"The food and all your supplies come to thirty dollars," she said.

His head shot up and his eyes began to twitch. That was a lot of money for his small list of supplies and one plate of food!

She looked at him without blinking. "Ned Black, that price includes me and my husband not seeing you here today, if someone comes asking."

He smiled. "That price is just fine, and I appreciate the good food and supplies."

She put everything in a gunnysack and handed it to him. He took it and walked out the door to his horse, where he tied the sack on his saddle horn and mounted up. He wanted to get out of that place and back on the road.

From the trading post, he rode northeast toward the Bennington Mission Station.

He would ride until about midnight before finding a camp spot. The farther he rode away from the river, the more the terrain became clustered with heavy growths of trees, brush, and large tangled briar thickets.

Ned had to slow down his pace the later and darker it got. His horse was tired, and he was tired and hungry again.

It was about ten that night when he thought he smelled smoke. He rode slowly, trying to locate where the scent was coming from. Just past a small grove of oak trees, he saw a light through the branches.

He rode that direction, and as he got closer, he figured out the light was coming through a window. It was the light of fire in a fireplace.

He rode in close and dismounted, tied his horse to a nearby tree and slowly walked up to the house, always staying in the shadows. It was a small, one-room shack with a cedar shake roof. He looked in the window, and there on the bed was an old man, sound asleep. He saw an empty bottle of whiskey on the floor. Ned smiled at his good fortune.

He eased the door open and walked into the room, pulling his gun out of the holster. He took it by the barrel and walked right up to the man and hit him on the crown of his head. Ned pulled the pillow out from under the man's head and put it over his face and finished off the job by smothering him to death.

When he was confident the man was dead, Ned pulled him off the bed, dragged him out of the house, and sat him outside against a porch post.

Ned went to his horse and led it to a small enclosure in back of the shack for the night. He removed the saddle and took it and his grub bag with him back into the house where it was warm.

He rummaged through the house looking for cooking utensils, he wanted to eat before he went to sleep. After heating up some of his food, he ate his supper then put more wood on the fire. It would be good to have some extra wood for the night, so he went outside and found the woodpile, bringing in an armful for the night. He looked at the man's bunk and decided he would lay his bedroll on it, since the blankets were filthy. He turned the feather mattress over before spreading out his covers.

By falling straight off to sleep, he never giving a moment's thought to killing the man.

When morning came, he warmed up his leftover food for breakfast, and then collected his belongings. He went out back, saddled his horse, tied his grub bag on and mounted. He rode around the front of the house to make sure the old man was still where he had left him. He looked like he was asleep.

Ned walked his horse back to the trail, never looking back.

It was another twenty miles to the Bennington Mission Station. If he continued at a decent pace, he could make it there by early afternoon. He rode on thinking about the time he had hid out there a few years back. He had been riding with Bill Anderson, and they were on the run from the law up in Kansas.

Bennington Mission Station was a school for Indian kids. The railroad came close by there, and the road was good from there east to Boswell. That was where Ned would turn north toward the mountains.

He rode hard and stopped one time for water and to rest his horse a few minutes. It was one in the afternoon when Ned rode into the little settlement of Bennington. He stopped at the store to see if they had any food prepared. The woman fixed him a beef sandwich out of sliced meat and soft white bread.

He ate the sandwich, mounted, and headed due east. He wanted to make Boswell by nightfall.

There was a hotel with a bar at Boswell where he planned to eat, drink, and spend the night. It would be a hard ride for his horse, but he pressed on as best he could, determined to sleep in a good, clean bed.

They made the ten miles to Boswell in good time, and stopped at the first livery stable he came to.

"Feed my horse some grain and hay and have him saddled shortly after daylight tomorrow," he told the stable hand.

"Yes sir, that'll be two dollars," said the man.

Ned handed the man two dollars and walked to the hotel. Once inside, he told the hotel clerk he wanted a good bed for the night and something to eat.

"We have beef stew and cornbread, or beef steak and taters with cornbread," the clerk said. "And that will be four dollars for the room. You pay for the food in the hotel eatery."

"Go tell the cook to get the steak going while I drop off my thigs," said Ned.

The clerk headed for the kitchen while Ned took his things to his room, and poured water from a pitcher into a wash bowl and washed his face and hands.

He went into the bar and took a seat at one of the tables. A woman who he suspected was the clerk's wife came over and asked, "What do you want to drink with your food, sir?"

"What are my choices?" he inquired.

"We have water, coffee, and some fresh chalk we keep cool down in the well. And we have some good corn whiskey."

"Bring me a shot of whiskey and a bucket of that cool chalk."

"Yes sir," she said.

She brought his drinks to the table, and a few minutes later she came with his food. It was a delicious meal. He finished up and was drinking the last of the chalk when he decided to have a little fun with her.

When she came to collect his empty plate she asked, "How did your food taste?"

"I'll tell you the truth, it was so good it would make a rabbit slap a dog." Ned laughed at his own remark, but she only smiled and walked off with his empty plate.

Well, that didn't go so well.

Ned had one more shot of whiskey and paid for his meal, then went to his room. He wanted to get an early start the next morning and try to make it to his hideout by nightfall. It was a good thirty miles, but he thought he could do it if everything worked out just right.

CHAPTER TWENTY-NINE

C ard left the Marshall's farm traveling in the direction Jacob had instructed. The terrain was not difficult. It was mostly flat land with a few rolling hills and some cultivated land. It seemed to be mostly a mix of farmland, timber, and brush.

He had ridden close to an hour when he came to a road that traveled east–west. He figured this was the road that Jacob had told him about and it would connect him to the road out of Paris heading to the Red River.

He passed a rider or wagon every once in a while, and they would exchange greetings and keep going. After another few hours he got hungry, so he found a small creek where Smoke could get a drink while he ate something. Card loosened the girth strap and let his horse graze, then found a tree under which he could sit. There he ate his sandwich and had water from his canteen, trying to keep his mind off Jean and the Marshall family. It was hard to do but he had to stay focused on what was ahead of him. He figured he could still be able to get to Ned's hideout before Ned, if things went as planned.

When he finished eating, he tightened up the girth strap and continued east in order to meet up with the road going north to the Red River.

In about an hour he found the north–south road he'd been looking for. He could tell from all the wagon wheel ruts and horse prints that it was heavily traveled. From there he was able to make good time on the road, and still hoped to get across the Red River before dark.

Everyone he passed by seemed friendly and would speak or touch their hat brim in greeting. Card did the same.

By late afternoon he came upon the Red River. There wasn't a ferry in operation at that particular location. He stopped at the riverbank and observed where the ferry had been in the past and wondered why there wasn't one in operation now, with all the traffic on the road. It looked too deep to cross on horseback, judging by the swift current of the water.

Card didn't want to get wet; the weather was too cold. He would need to find another place to cross.

Parked to the east were a couple of wagons. It looked like a camp of some sort, that had been there for a while. He rode toward the small group.

There appeared to be two families camped together and sharing a large fire. From the look of their clothes and living conditions, as well as the condition of their wagons, Card figured they had experienced some hard times.

"Can I come into your camp?" asked Card as he rode closer.

"Come on in, iffn' you're friendly," a man said. "We don't want no trouble and don't have anything of value."

Card rode into their camp. "I'm needing to cross the river; do you know a good place where I can ford without getting too wet?"

The man pointed to the east and said, "The water is shallow down yonder. We took our wagons through there three days ago without any trouble, and it's no more than belly deep for your horse. It may be a little swift, but you shouldn't have any trouble."

"Thanks," said Card. He started off in the direction the man had pointed.

It wasn't long until he found the spot. He guided Smoke down the riverbank and into the water. Card took his boots out of the stirrups and coaxed Smoke into the cold water. It wasn't deep and Smoke walked through it without any difficulty. On the other side it was all wash sand, and Smoke had a little trouble getting through but once they were out of the riverbed, the ground was firm and covered with dead grass.

Card was glad to be on the north side of the river and in Indian Territory. This was the first time he had ever been on this side of Red River.

He rode back to the road and increased Smoke's speed. It was getting near night, and he would need to find a suitable campsite for the night. He had ridden a few miles when he saw a house to the northeast through some trees. He wondered if they would let him sleep in their barn.

He rode that way and sure enough, it was a little house with a barn and corral, in front of a large, cultivated field.

He stopped in front of the house and alerted the people inside that they had company.

A large Black man opened the door and peered out. "Who's out there?" he shouted. "Come on in where I can see you."

Card rode toward the house, closer to the front door.

"Sir, my name is Card Jordan," he said. "I'm trailing a murderer and need a place to bed down with some shelter for the night. I am hoping I can sleep in your barn. I won't be any trouble or anything, and I can pay you for letting me stay."

"Are you a lawman?" the man asked.

"No sir, that man and his gang killed my family and I'm going after him to make him pay."

"Okay then. I reckon you're telling the truth. Put your horse in the corral and come on to the house. My wife is setting the table for supper, and we've got plenty. That is, if you don't mind eating with Black folk."

"That'd be great, and I don't care what color a person's skin is," said Card.

He took Smoke to the barn and removed the saddle before turning the horse loose in the corral. Card found a pitchfork and put hay in the feed trough.

He thought about leaving his gun with his things in the barn, but that could be a mistake.

He knocked on the door before opening it and walking in. He could see only three rooms in the house: a kitchen, a living room, and one bedroom.

"Come on into the kitchen," said the man. "I'm John Henry Webb, and this is my wife, Mary Webb."

Card shook their hands and told them again, "I'm Card Jordan, from Red River County, Texas."

"Take a seat," said Mary. "I hope you like fried squirrel, turnip greens, black eyed peas, and cornbread."

"I certainly do, and I appreciate the food. It smells delicious," said Card.

John Henry said a prayer before they started eating.

"This squirrel sure is good," Card said. "And I really appreciate you inviting me in to eat."

"We don't get much company out here, so it's good to have someone to talk to," she said. "Other than John Henry all the time."

They laughed at her remark.

"I don't know why she would say something like that, I usually can't get a word in edgewise from her talking all the time," said John Henry.

They ate in silence for a while before Card asked. "Do you know where Goodland is?"

"Yep, you stay on the main road for about eight miles from here," said John Henry. "There's a sign that points to the west. Follow the road about two miles and you can't miss it."

"I'm going to stop there for some supplies tomorrow," said Card. "I'm heading up the Kiamichi River to the Moyers mountains, and don't know how long it'll take me to get there. I'll need to stock up on supplies in case I'm there for a while."

"If you stay on the main road, you'll come to a bigger settlement than Goodland. It's got a couple different stores and such, and it's only a few more miles north," John Henry said.

"That sounds good, thanks," said Card.

After supper Card told them, "I'm sure grateful for the food and for you letting me use the barn to sleep in tonight."

They exchanged goodnights and Card went to the barn, unrolled his bedroll, put it on the hay, and got comfortable for a good night's sleep.

CHAPTER THIRTY

Ned was on the trail immediately after sunrise. He was bundled up and riding into a strong north wind. He went northeast until he came to Clear Boggy Creek. It looked deep, so he rode up the creek a little way until he found a suitable place to ford.

Once across, it was slow going for his horse until they rode clear of the soft creek bottom.

North a few miles he came to Muddy Boggy Creek. It was more like a small river than a big creek. With a little searching, Ned managed to find a place to cross where he wouldn't get wet.

Once clear of the two creeks he sped up his horse and continued on.

The land was beginning to open up some, becoming prairie and rolling hills. He suspected he was getting close to the little settlement of Nelson. He had killed a man there a year earlier, so he decided to ride clear of it, just in case anyone saw him and decided to put a bullet in his back.

Instead of following the road into town, Ned gave it a wide berth and crossed the road that connected Nelson to a town to the east. Then he knew he was clear of the settlement.

He splashed through small streams and across pastures where cattle were grazing. This part of Indian Territory had an abundance of large trees and wildlife. He noticed where loggers had left bare stumps scattered throughout the countryside.

He finally came to the road that ran from Kuniotubbee west to Atoka, in Indian Territory.

This was now the last leg of his journey before reaching his hideout in the mountains.

But first he needed to stop and rest his horse and eat; Coffee Creek wasn't far ahead, and it would be a good place to go.

He found a campsite that he was familiar with; he'd used it many times in the past. There was good clear water, grass for his horse, and shelter for himself. He built a small fire and put water from the creek in his coffee pot. While waiting on it to boil, he ate some jerky and cold biscuits he had bought in Boswell.

All of a sudden, the wind picked up and it began to get colder.

He stood up and walked to one end of his camp so he could look through the trees to the north. The clouds in the sky was turning a grayish blue in color. Ned stomped his foot in disgust and said a few choice curse words. This wasn't what he wanted right now.

A blue northern was blowing in and it was going to get extremely cold, very fast. He checked the progress of his coffee; it wasn't as strong as he liked it, but it'd have to do. He had one cup, then poured the remaining drink on the fire and mounted up.

Ned knew he would have to push his horse hard now, to make it to the shack before the weather got much colder. He rode north and followed a trail that led to the Kiamichi River. The terrain was changing rapidly to rocks and pine trees, with only a few hardwoods scattered in.

His horse was laboring hard from swerving around the rocks and boulders that lined the trail, but Ned still couldn't afford to stop. They crossed Frederick Creek and continued on without resting.

By now he was cold to the bone. The wind was blowing hard and he needed to get out of this weather, fast.

Along the next creek he came to after turning in a westerly direction, he found a rock ledge that could protect him from the wind. He would let his horse rest until he was breathing regular again. They would be climbing higher soon so he knew his horse would need his strength to make it to the shack. At least the shack was less than two miles away now.

After resting his horse a few more minutes, Ned continued west until he found the spot where Wildhorse Creek combined with another smaller creek. He crossed Wildhorse Creek and rode around a large boulder. On the back side of the boulder was a deer trail that went up the mountain and he followed it until he came to two more boulders, about three feet apart. He turned in between them and a short distance later he found his shack.

On one side of the shack was a small corral about

twenty feet wide by eighty feet long. It was built years ago out of small trees and branches. The back of the corral was a rock wall with a partial cave in it that would shelter the horse. Ned untied his provision sack and unsaddled his horse, then turned him into the corral. A little stream flowed through the corner of the enclosure so his horse would have plenty of water, and winter grass grew in clumps scattered throughout for him to eat. On nice days Ned would stake him out on other spots of grass to eat but for now he had plenty where he was.

Ned carried his provision sack with him to the shack. He opened the door and looked around before entering, to make sure some varmint hadn't taken up residence. It looked clear and he went in, deciding to take his chances. He put his provisions on the table and started a fire in the fireplace. There was still wood in the wood box, from when he had been there earlier in the year.

While the fire caught, he went outside to get his saddle so it would be out of the elements.

It was getting bitterly cold outside now. He didn't want to go back out again but decided to bring in more firewood for the night. Maybe enough for tomorrow, too. He went to the wood pile outside by the rock wall.

Ned brought in an abundance of wood, then he took another good look around the shack.

It had been built in front of another small cave in the side of the rock wall. This cave went back about eight feet. The rock wall faced to the south and was about thirty feet high. It protected the shack from the cold north wind. A small stream of water seeped out of the rocks, providing fresh water. Someone had carved out a basin in the rock floor so it could fill with water before flowing outside.

The cave was large enough for a couple of bunks. He went to his bunk, picked up his bedding, and shook it out. Dust filled the air. He took his coffee pot to the basin and filled it with water before placing it in the fireplace to heat up.

Next, he found the water bucket and filled it. Using an old rag, he cleaned off the grime that had accumulated on what furniture there was.

By the time the coffee was ready, it had begun to warm up in the shack and Ned settled in for the night.

CHAPTER THIRTY-ONE

C ard woke up to the sun coming in through the cracks in the barn wall. He got up and gathered his things, then saddled up Smoke so he would be ready to be on his way.

John Henry came to the barn door and said, "Come on to the house, breakfast is ready."

Card followed him inside. There was more fried squirrel, biscuits, gravy, and hot strong coffee.

"You need another hot meal before you start out today," said Mary.

"I never turn down good food and good company," said Card.

John Henry, do you own this place and the farmland behind it?"

"No sir, I share crop for Mr. Richardson," he said. "He's a hard man to get along with, but it provides us a house and food to eat and enough money to get by on."

"Are you a good farmer?" asked Card.

"He's a very good farmer. He can plow all day long with his pair of Missouri mules," said Mary proudly.

Card smiled and asked, "If you had the opportunity to work at a really good place, would the two of you consider moving to Texas?"

John Henry looked at Mary and said, "Yes sir, I do believe we would."

Nodding his head, Card shook hands with John Henry. Then he walked over to Mary and gave her a big hug and took hold of her hand. He had twenty dollars folded up in his palm, and he placed it in her hand. She looked at it and smiled broadly, touching him on his cheek with her slender fingers.

After he mounted his horse, he headed back to the road. Once there, he put Smoke into a lope until he got to a creek, where he let Smoke cool down and have his fill of water.

He continued north and saw the sign for the road that went to Goodland. He went past it and continued to the other settlement John Henry had told him about. Guiding Smoke to the hitch rail in front of the store, he dismounted and went inside to stock up on provisions. Not knowing how long it would take to find Ned, he wanted plenty of grub in case he was in the mountains longer than he had planned for.

The place was more than a settlement. It was a small town with two stores, a hotel, a diner, and a few other places of business.

After telling the clerk what he needed, he milled around inside one of the stores while his order got filled. Two middle-aged men entered and demanded, "We want some Cotton Boll Twist chewing tobacco, five pounds of bacon, and three pounds of beans. And be quick about it."

The clerk said with a shaky voice, "I'm filling this feller's order right now, I'll be with you directly."

One of the men pulled his coat back to reveal his gun. "I don't reckon you heard my friend with those stopped-up ears of yours," he said to the clerk. "Maybe I need to unstop 'em for you."

Card eased around a table stacked high with clothing. He removed the leather safety off his gun and stepped out in front of the men.

"You fellows will wait your turn. I was here first, and I'm not a patient man," said Card.

Now both men had their coats pulled open for access to their guns and one of them said, "Boy, we ain't going to spend time messing with you. You are about to feel the wrath of Ellis Wilson and David Fellows."

Card laughed. His hand palmed his gun and had it pointed at them before they even knew what was happening.

Card said, "It seems to me that you two need to learn some manners. When someone tells you they'll be with you in a few minutes, you need to wait your turn."

Both men were staring at the gun pointed at them.

The bigger of the two said, "If you weren't holding that gun, I'd take you out in the street and give you a beating your daddy should be doing, boy."

Card eased his gun back into the holster. "I'll oblige you, since you are so willing to teach me a free lesson," Card said. "We'll go out into the street and have school."

The three men went out the door and down the steps of the store. Card kicked the man who challenged him to a fight out into the street. The other one started to turn around to throw a fist at Card, but was stopped short by the business end of a double-barrel shotgun held by the store clerk.

"Ellis started this and he's the only one who's going to fight this man," said the clerk to David.

David hollered to Ellis, who was on his hands and knees. "Get up and teach this boy a lesson!"

Ellis stood up, pulled off his coat, and threw it on the porch.

Standing with his hands shielding his face, Card was ready to throw a punch or block one.

His pa had given him lessons from an early age on hand-to-hand combat. He had passed on to his son all that he had been taught while serving in the Army.

Card advanced forward to get closer to Ellis, who then threw a wide punch with his right hand.

Card ducked under the fist and stepped in close enough to deliver a solid blow to Ellis' stomach. The man made the mistake of dropping his arms while trying to draw in air.

Card took the opportunity to hit him with a roundhouse right that landed on his jaw, causing his head to turn sideways.

Ellis made one more attempt to inflict pain on his opponent and threw a haymaker that landed on Card's left arm. Card grimaced with pain—Ellis had hit him in the same shoulder he'd been shot in. Nonetheless, he reacted with a punch of his own. He hit Ellis on the side of his nose. The blood flowed freely from Ellis's nostrils and his eyes were watering so badly. He wiped at his eyes to clear out the tears.

Another thing Card noticed and took advantage of.

He quickly stepped in with another blow to the man's midsection and followed it with a punch to the face.

Ellis collapsed to the ground, out cold.

Card stood looking down at him and rubbed his shoulder. He looked at David and asked, "Are we good now, since I've whipped your partner?"

"Yep, we're good," said David in a terse tone.

David went to Ellis. He bent down and slapped his partner on the cheek. Ellis opened his eyes in confusion. "You boys help me up, I'm a little shaky," he said.

Card stuck out his hand and Ellis grabbed it. Card and David heaved the dazed man up and onto his feet. He stood on shaky legs and rubbed his chin. "You pack a mighty good punch, young man," he said. "I ain't been knocked out in a long time."

Card was still rubbing his shoulder. "You've got some power yourself," he admitted.

"David, help me over to Jim's place," said Ellis. "I need a strong drink to clear my head."

Card went back into the store and collected his supplies.

"That was some fight, mister. Those two are both bullies around here," said the clerk.

"Sometimes a man has to stand up to people like that," said Card.

He got back on his way after loading his supplies and rode until the sun was high overhead.

Finally, he stopped to rest Smoke and eat some jerky and cold bread he bought at the store.

Then he was back on the road again, allowing Smoke to move along at an easy pace. The terrain was changing; the hardwood trees were thinning out to give way to tall pines and the ground had become rocky. He crossed numerous creeks and streams. It was midafternoon by the time he came to an east–west road. He figured it was the road that headed west out of Kuniotubbee but wasn't sure which way to go before he needed to turn north. He searched the horizon in both directions and saw a wagon coming from the east. He waited until the wagon was close, then put his hand up to see if they would stop.

"Good afternoon, sir," said Card. "I'm trying to find where Frederick Creek runs into the Kiamichi River. You wouldn't by chance know which way I need to go to get there, would you?"

"Yep, you go west about another quarter of a mile," said the man. "There you'll see a trail that goes north. You follow that all the way to the big bend in the river and the creek is only about a mile north of there."

"Thanks for the information and you have a good day," said Card, touching the brim of his hat.

The man slapped the reins to the hindquarters of his horses and continued west.

Card waited to let the wagon get ahead of him, then he went west also, looking for the trail the man had told him about.

He made good time due to the condition of the

trail. He began to feel more confident until he noticed the wind had picked up and it was getting colder.

He stopped long enough to untie his heavy coat and put it on. He checked the sky several times as he rode north. The clouds had turned a grayish blue, and he knew what was going to happen. A blue northern was blowing in and it would become dangerously cold soon. He would have to find shelter and wait it out.

He kept riding until he saw a rock wall facing south, with an overhang that might be large enough to provide protection for both him and Smoke. He rode toward it, weaving around boulders.

When he reached the overhang, he tied Smoke so he could graze on some winter grass while he gathered firewood. By the time he had an abundance of wood stacked against the rock wall, the temperature had dropped even more, and the wind was bitter.

He tied his tarp between some trees growing close to the side of the wall, hoping it would help to keep the wind out.

Pa had taught him to build a fire close to rocks, so they would get hot and help keep him warm.

He poured water from his canteen to boil for coffee while he unsaddled Smoke. The ground was going to get cold soon, so Card gathered leaves, grass, and pine needles to lay his saddle blanket and tarp on. He placed his bedroll on top of it all, and hoped it'd be soft enough to sleep on the hard rock. He was all set for a cold night, now to cook some supper. He knew a full stomach would also help keep him warm.

It was well below freezing by the time morning came. Card got out of his bed, put more wood on the fire and reheated the coffee from the night before. He sat leaning against his saddle with his covers around his shoulders. The wind was blowing about thirty miles an hour, the sky was over-cast. He knew he would have to wait until the cold front moved out. There was no way he could find Ned's hideout in this kind of weather.

Around three that afternoon, the wind finally died down and the sun came out. Card could tell the difference in the temperature almost immediately. He collected Smoke and led him to the shelter to put the saddle on him. He rolled up his bedroll and secured it along with his grub bag and travel bag to the saddle, then mounted. He rode back to the road and continued north. Navigating rocky trails was something new to Smoke, and Card didn't want his horse to get injured, so he let the horse walk at his own pace. Card could see the Kiamichi River to his right when he rode upon another creek. This creek had to be Frederick Creek, based on the description Bill had given him.

Card crossed through the water and started up the other side of the bank. There he saw tracks made by a horse.

He continued on north and every once in a while, he'd see a full horse track or sometimes a partial one.

It was almost dark when he came to a much larger creek. It was the biggest one he'd seen so far and from the directions the man on the road and Bill had given him, this had to be Buck Creek. This was where he would turn west and follow the creek up the mountain.

It was late now, and he needed to find a good place to spend the night. Up the creek a little way were some boulders scattered on a flat shelf of ground. Card rode to the boulders; they would make a good campsite.

He piled up some smaller rocks in a semicircle in which to build a fire. The smaller rocks close to the fire would help keep him warm. He unsaddled Smoke and ground tied him close by. Card cooked and ate his supper, then he sat evaluating his gun skills. It seemed that he had a gift when it came to drawing his weapon. He had outdrawn six men so far. His confidence was beginning to overcome the fear he had first started out with. He wasn't scared of Ned Black. Ned was just a varmint that had to be killed.

Bundled in his blankets, he laid listening to the fire crackle and thought about what tomorrow might bring. Ned was close by; he could feel it in his aching bones. Starting tomorrow he would be extra careful. Ned could be behind any boulder along the trail, waiting to shoot him in the back.

CHAPTER THIRTY-TWO

Ned added extra wood to the fireplace before he went to bed. He got up twice during the night to add more wood. The old shack was not insulated and had gaps between the boards, but it kept enough heat in to stay comfortable.

It was well after daylight when Ned got out of bed and put coffee on to boil. He looked outside and noticed that the stream that flowed through the corral was frozen over. Great. Now he would have to go out in the cold to chop a hole in the ice later so his horse could drink.

He drank coffee for a while then cooked his breakfast. When he finished, he prepared a pot of red beans with bacon for seasoning and hung it on the swivel arm inside the fireplace to cook. It would make a good supper. He figured on staying inside most of the day where it was warm, until the cold spell moved out.

Late that afternoon he finally went outside and chopped holes in the ice so his horse could get to fresh water. The sky was clearing off and the sun was out. Tomorrow he would get out and have a look around. Bill might be coming soon.

If Bill does show up, I'll kill him, take what money he has left, and go somewhere warm. He'd already had it with the cold.

After he brought in more wood for the fireplace, he washed his hands and sat down to eat his beans and bacon.

About eight or so that night, he began to think about going to bed. He went outside to relieve himself and smelled a weak whiff of smoke. The wind was out of the southeast and he stood where he was, looking down the mountain for any light from a fire. Concerned, he stayed outside until he got too cold.

"Oh well, maybe I'm just imagining things," he mumbled.

He went back inside and instead of going right to bed, he decided to clean his guns. On an old piece of blanket laid out on the table, he disassembled his guns. Then he got a small tin of gun oil out of his saddlebags along with a cleaning rag. He wiped all the parts with the rag and used a small rod to push a small piece of cloth through the barrels. When he finished and had his guns reassembled, he operated the mechanisms to be sure they functioned correctly.

Waking up early the next morning, he made coffee and ate some of the beans and bacon for breakfast. Still concerned, he couldn't get the fact he'd smelled smoke out of his mind, even though he never could see a fire below.

Maybe he should watch the path coming up the

mountain and the surrounding area along the creek for a while. If someone was out there, he would see from his high advantage point. He gathered up his warm coat and rifle and went out into the brisk morning air. There was a location where he could see all the way down the mountain side, where Wildhorse Creek flowed into Buck Creek. He went on foot to a large boulder that had rolled down from somewhere above years ago. It was easy to climb on top of it and look around. As he sat on the boulder scanning the area below, he spotted a man on a horse riding slowly coming up along the creek. The man was bent over, looking at the ground as if searching for something. Every few feet he would stop and look around, then continue on slowly.

Ned rested on his stomach on top of the boulder, so the rider couldn't see him. With his rifle laying in front of him and in position to shoot, he let the stranger get closer before he did anything. From that distance, Ned couldn't tell who it was, but he would be ready when the man got within shooting range. If it was Bill, he would kill him and take his money. That'd be enough for him to live nicely until spring in some faraway place.

CHAPTER THIRTY-THREE

Card awakened with his back and joints hurting from lying on the hard, cold makeshift bed. The grass and leaves he had used under his bedroll was not near enough padding. At least it was already warmer than it had been the day before. He got up and began to bend and move his arms and shoulders, trying to make his joints feel better. After loosening up his aching body he moved some coals around on the fire and added a couple of sticks to get the flames blazing. Sitting close to the flames, he ate the leftovers from the night before with a fresh cup of coffee. When he was finished, he gathered up all his belongings and saddled Smoke. He poured out the remaining coffee on his fire and loaded his bags. Maybe today would be the day he'd find Ned. He mounted and started back up the creek.

Card took the trail slower than usual, searching for horse tracks and watching for any place that could provide a good cover for someone to bushwhack him.

Every few feet he paused long enough to look around carefully.

He rode around some rocks blocking the trail and saw where another creek ran into the creek he was following. He stopped, and surveyed the area, then crossed the creek. He saw a large boulder and thought, *the trail to Ned's hideout must be here somewhere.*

He bent over to look at the ground just as a gunshot rang out. The bullet whined past his head and hit a nearby rock, spewing fragments of stone at him and Smoke. Kicking his feet free from the stirrups, he dove to the ground and scrambled for cover. He couldn't tell exactly where the shot had come from.

Smoke walked up the trail and found some clumps of grass to eat while Card stood close to the boulder. It seemed like thirty minutes before he moved slightly away to see if the shooter was still there. He couldn't see anything, so he took a step away from his shelter. Another bullet ricocheted off the hard surface making a loud whine.

Card fired two quick shots back, still not seeing anything. Ned or one of his friends are up there somewhere trying to kill him, and Card needed a way to get from where he was and advance on the shooter.

The shooter holler down to him, "Bounty hunter, I'm going to kill you today."

"I'm not a bounty hunter," Card hollered back. "I'm here to kill a murderer and a thief.

"Come on up here and we will settle this eye-to-eye," he yelled.

Card laughed. "You want me to walk up there, out in the open, so we can settle this?"

"Yep," said the shooter. "I give you my word, I won't shoot you until we can do this standing in front of each other."

"I'll make you the same offer," said Card. "You come down here and I'll give you a chance to kill me face to face. That is, if you've got the guts."

Card eased around his cover, hoping to get on its backside where he could see better and maybe advance up the trail. When he finally got to the other side, he saw he'd have to cross about ten feet of open ground before there was more cover. He could see the trail that would lead him up to the hideout.

He waited, looking around for any movement above him. He took one step forward and the rifle fired again. This time the bullet was so close it tore the material on the left arm of his coat. Card took cover again and waited. How could he get up that trail? He wished he had his Winchester; it would give him more fire power. But it was in his saddle-boot.

Card hugged the side of the large rock. When he tried to make a move, another bullet hit the stone and shattered off shards of rock. One of the shards hit Card in his right cheek and opened up a small gash. He rubbed his cheek and saw the blood. He pulled out his handkerchief and held it to his face.

Card said in a whisper, "Pa, that was close, I can sure use a little more help. He has me pinned down and I don't see how I'm going to get up that trail without getting shot. I don't even know where he is located. I have been patient, but time is on his side right now."

CHAPTER THIRTY-FOUR

Ned knew what he was up against. This young gunfighter was fast and accurate and had proven that by killing all his men. The kid was getting under Ned's skin. For the first time in his life, he did not want to face up to the gunman hiding behind the boulder. He decided to wait until he had another shot. If he hit him, great. And if he didn't, he would hurry back to the shack, saddle his horse, and load up his stuff. Then he'd come back and fire another shot at the boy before riding out the back way. Being a careful man, he always had an escape route out of a hideout and it would hopefully take the gunman the rest of the day to figure out he was gone.

Taking aim, Ned fired a shot and took off to the shack. He went inside and packed up the things he wanted to take with him and put the sack outside the door.

Ned ran back and forth, between his hideout and

the boulder, firing shots at the gunman until he had his horse saddled and ready to travel.

On his last trip back to fire a shot, he saw movement and fired, hitting Card's hat. Good enough, he thought, and ran to his horse where he then rode up the mountain for about a hundred feet before turning east. There was an old animal path that would take him down and around the back side of the rock wall where the shack was. He let his horse have his head and follow the trail. It would eventually come out on the road down by the river that he had ridden in on.

CHAPTER THIRTY-FIVE

Card took hold of the brim of his hat and slid it around the rock, placing it in the line of fire. A shot rang out from up above, and he jerked his hat back. There was a large hole in his pa's Calvary hat. That made two holes that had been put in the hat by Ned or one of his men. There wasn't going to be a third.

Without knowing where the shooter was, Card waited and watched. It'd been close to an hour since the bullet had penetrated his hat. He had to move and get closer to the hideout and the only way was to run as hard as he could while shooting blindly up the mountain. When he was ready, he took off, firing as rapidly as his finger could pull the trigger. When safely on the deer trail, he reloaded his gun and walked up the narrow path, keeping behind cover as much as possible. The terrain slowed him down; the ground was littered with rocks and stones that rolled under his riding boots.

A column of smoke was rising into the air, and it had to be coming from the shack. He knew he was getting close and decided to leave the trail in case it was being watched.

By climbing higher up the mountain, he would be able to see the hideout clearer. The corral gate was down and there was no horse around. Whoever had been shooting at him must have taken off, but since he wasn't sure, he still had to be careful. He worked his way down to the cabin.

Card ran to the front door and kicked it in, then went inside with his gun drawn. It was empty, and he could tell someone had left in a hurry. There was a pot of beans still on the hearth of the fireplace and the coffee pot was setting on the table. No one leaves without their coffee pot, although he did take his bedroll since the bunks had no bedding on them.

So, it was Ned that was shooting at him and now he is on the run again. All he grabbed was his bedroll, and left most of his food supplies. That meant he was not planning on going very far.

Card walked back down the trail to find Smoke and brought him back up to the shack and put him in the corral. There was still a chill in the mountain air, so he went inside and took the pot of beans away from the fire and found a spoon and began to eat. No point letting good food go to waste.

When he was finished eating, he walked outside and surveyed the area.

"If it was me, which way would I go?" he said aloud, then paused for a moment. "I'd go north, up the mountain."

He walked in that direction while watching for a chipped-off rock, a hoofprint, a broken twig; any sign that a horse or man had disturbed the ground.

He walked about two hundred feet, then stopped. The terrain was getting rougher, and it'd be difficult for a horse and rider to go any farther.

Card turned around and looked back the way he had come. Then he saw it—berries from a cedar tree scattered on the ground. Someone must have brushed the tree as they went by, knocking the berries off. He walked to the tree and turned east, going between some large rocks. He found an old animal trail and followed it until he could see the back side of the rock wall where the shack was located.

The old trail headed down the mountain toward the river. He knew where Ned was going. Right back to the road he came in on.

Card walked back to the shack and went inside to look at the supplies that were left behind and considered who Ned was and what he was capable of.

Ned was a coward when he was face-to-face with his opponent. He was the kind of man who murdered innocent men, women, and kids, or bushwhacked unaware travelers. He wanted everyone to fear him, and that was why he wore black clothes and carried that fancy gun.

Card found an old sack which he took outside and filled with pine cones and pine needles. He went back in the shack and put the table against the wall, then pulled the bunks out of the cave and put them on top of the table. He threw all the firewood against the table. There was bacon grease left in the skillet, so he heated it up and poured it on the wood. When he was ready, he stuck the sack into the fireplace. It caught on fire, and he tossed it onto the wood, igniting the bacon grease and the flames began climbing up the wall, spreading up to the roof.

Card walked outside to his horse and mounted. No outlaw would ever use this place as a hideout again.

He headed back the way he'd come up the mountain, since he was familiar with that route and could make better time.

CHAPTER THIRTY-SIX

Ned traversed down the mountain to the same trail he had ridden in on. Then he put his heels to his horse and tried to put distance between himself and the bounty hunter. Once satisfied with his escape, it was time to decide where he would go next. A plan began to form in his mind. He would ride hard past Kuniotubbee for a few miles until he got to Joe's Trading Post. A critical part of the strategy was to leave a trail so the gunman would follow him to Joe's. For $500, he could get Joe to blow the boy away with his double-barrel shotgun when he came through the door of the trading post.

After making the deal with Joe, he would turn southeast and ride to Gilbert, Indian Territory, where he would sell his horse and saddle, buy new clothes, get a haircut and shave, and buy a new gun. His pearl-handled gun was a dead giveaway of his identity. It would go in his bag so no one would see it.

Probably no one would recognize him when he

was cleaned up and wearing new clothes, especially the gunman, since he'd never seen him up close. Hopefully he never would, if Joe's shotgun did its job.

From Gilbert he could catch a train on The Arkansas and Choctaw railroad and take it to Arkansas. And maybe even farther east.

When he came up to the main road that would take him to Kuniotubbee, he slowed his horse to a walk. Even though he had a plan to kill the bounty hunter. He still wanted to be careful and put distance between them by having his horse tracks blend in with the rest of the tracks on the road. He turned east and continued to walk his horse for a distance of 100 yards, then he slapped him with the reins and had him back to a run.

As he went up the hill into the settlement, he walked his horse again, not wanting to draw attention to his presence. There was a group of Indians over by the spring filling buckets with water, but he stayed clear of them.

When he was past all the dwellings, he ran his horse until he came to Cedar Creek. He only slowed down long enough to cross the water and then ran his horse again.

His horse was getting winded from the constant exertion, so Ned slowed him to a walk. Joe's Trading Post had to be close by, so it was time to intentionally lead the gunman there. He eased to the edge of the road and increased the pace, making his tracks easy to follow.

Ned arrived at the trading post and dismounted in front of the old false-fronted building. He led his horse around to the back so the gunman could see his boot tracks, then left his horse out back and went inside the store.

Joe greeted Ned. "How are you doing, old friend?" He poured Ned a shot of shine and set it on the counter.

Ned emptied the glass and motioned for another. "I need a favor," Ned said. "I've got a bounty man after me and I'll give you $500 to blow him away with your double-barrel when he comes in here looking for me."

Ned drained the second glass of shine and blew air out of his mouth.

"That's some mighty fine shine, ain't it, Ned?" said Joe, laughing. "Now, about this favor you want. What does this bounty man look like?"

"He's young and riding a gray horse. He wears an old Calvary hat and he's fast with his gun, so don't let him suspect anything," said Ned. "When he walks through that door, you blast him with both barrels of that sawed-off shotgun you've got under the counter."

"All right, I'll do it," said Joe. "Now give me my money."

Ned paid him and started toward the door when Joe called out, "Ned, you forgot to pay for your drinks." Ned flipped him a silver dollar and went out the back door to his horse.

He rode in the grass until he came back to the road, where he mixed his tracks with all the other tracks.

After riding about a half mile, there was an area beside the road where the grass was high enough to hide his tracks. He turned south and continued to walk his horse for about a quarter of a mile. The terrain was opening up to pastureland with scattered groves of trees.

Urging his horse into a fast lope, he rode through shallow streams, groves of trees, and more pastureland. He wanted to get as far as possible and hopefully all the way to Salt Creek, even if he had to ride on after dark.

CHAPTER THIRTY-SEVEN

C ard rode down the mountain trail and went toward the main road. He hadn't ridden far when he saw where a horse had come off the side of the mountain and onto the road. From there it had run south down the trail. He suspected it was Ned's horse making the tracks.

He continued south, following the hoof prints. When he reached the main road, he couldn't tell which way Ned went. Card got off his horse and walked slowly to the west, looking for Ned's tracks. After a short distance walking west, he decided Ned had not gone that way, so he turned around and walked toward the east. A few yards down the road he found a track that resembled Ned's horse print. He kept following that track until he saw where the horse had begun to run. The tracks were deeper and the distance between hoof prints was farther apart. Card walked back to Smoke, mounted, and followed the tracks of the running horse. It wasn't long until they came to a set of train tracks going north and south. It looked like the horse's trail stopped here, or he had slowed to a walk.

There were so many tracks in the road now that Card couldn't figure out which ones belonged to Ned. He figured Ned had slowed to a walk through the small settlement. At the top of a hill where a cluster of buildings and in between the store and bank, he saw people getting water out of a spring and rode to them.

"Have any of you seen a man wearing black clothes riding a horse along here?" he asked.

An Indian boy about ten said, "He went that way." He pointed to the east.

Card thanked him and flipped him a quarter before riding back to the road.

He figured Ned was trying to be careful and blend his horse's tracks in with the other tracks, to throw him off his trail.

After riding slowly for about a mile, he came to a creek and crossed a shallow stream. No more than fifty feet from the creek he saw where a horse had begun to run. His gut feeling told him those tracks belong to Ned and that he was running his horse again.

Card picked up his pace enough that he could still make out the other horse tracks. But it wasn't long until he lost them again. He rode a little farther and came to another creek. It had steep banks, so he had to look closely to find where Ned had crossed. He rode north but saw no indication that a horse had been that way, he turned around and rode south and found where people forded the creek.

When he was on the other side and on flat ground

again, he found the tracks of a running horse. It looked like it was someone in a big hurry, so he suspected it was Ned. The trail was easy to follow for a distance, until he could see where the horse had begun to slow to a walk, and the tracks blended in with all the other traffic on the road.

Card stopped to rest Smoke and eat some jerky. After a few minutes he mounted again and rode back the way he'd come for a little way. He noticed a lone set of tracks at the edge of the road. How had he missed these?

As he rode alongside the tracks, scanning the roadside for an ambush, he started to understand what might be going on. Ned was familiar with this part of the country and he was up to something. The outlaw was too careful to leave his tracks in plain view like this.

Card rode another three hundred yards and saw a building with a sign on the false front: *Joe's Trading Post.*

He followed the tracks all the way to the trading post and saw where the rider had dismounted in the front of the building and then led the horse around to the back.

Right then and there, Card knew it was a trap. He removed the safety strap from his gun as he dismounted, keeping his horse between himself and the trading post in case Ned was waiting on him inside. He walked his horse around to the back, but didn't see Ned's horse anywhere, but he could tell someone had ridden away.

He had intentionally wanted Card to follow his

tracks, so he must've set something up inside the trading post.

Card removed his coat off his saddle and eased back around to the front of the building. He stood as far as he could to the side of the door while still being able to reach the handle. Then he leaned over and jerked the door open and threw the coat inside.

The blast from a double-barrel shotgun propelled the coat back out the door and away from the building. Card stepped through the door to find a man trying to reload his firearm, so he pulled his own pistol and shot the man just as he was closing the chamber and bringing the weapon up into a shooting position.

The man lay on the dirt floor moaning in pain from a wound in his chest. Card walked to him and searched him for another gun.

The man said, "I was too greedy, I guess. You done shot me."

"Did Ned Black put you up to this?" asked Card.

"Yeah, he paid me five hundred dollars. It's over yonder under the washtub."

Card walked to a washtub that was turned upside down. He bent down to lift it up, but something warned him not to. He saw a shovel leaning against the wall and stuck it under the brim of the tub and heaved it over.

There was a diamondback rattlesnake, coiled and ready to strike

Card drew his gun and shot its head off.

He smiled and said, "Mama, I do believe that was you warning me this time."

He walked back to the man, who was now dead.

Card looked around the store and saw a coat made from cowhide hanging on the wall. He tried it on. It fit nicely, and since his coat was shot through with buckshot, he'd take this one.

Then he walked outside, mounted his horse, and continued east. It wasn't far before he found Ned's tracks again. The dirt was torn up from him running his horse.

A hundred feet farther and the tracks went away completely. Had he left the road?

Card got about thirty feet off the north side of the road and rode alongside it. At first, he thought Ned might be going back up into the mountains, but after riding about a mile, he didn't see any signs this had happened. Card crossed over to the south side of the road and rode back the direction he'd come.

He had ridden about three-quarters of a mile when he saw grass that had been pressed down by horse hooves.

Card turned south and followed the imprints in the grass. It wasn't long until the tracks started spreading out. Ned was running his horse again. It was mostly pastureland with scattered trees now, so he'd been able to run fast. He knew Ned wouldn't be able to keep going at this pace all day; he would have to stop and rest his horse somewhere, at some point.

Card crossed streams and made his way around shallow swampy patches. It seemed like the ground was getting softer from all the wetness in the area. By late afternoon he knew he would have to find a good camp for the night. His horse needed rest and something to eat and so did he.

He came upon a good-sized creek with running water and winter grass in the timber that lined the creek bank. He decided to spend the night there. After he finished his supper and got in his bedroll for the night, he wondered where Ned might be going and what was he up too.

Ned knew this country fairly well and he had friends who were dangerous. Was he planning another ambush? Was he trying to escape to another hideout? These were all questions that Card couldn't answer so he finally drifted off to sleep.

CHAPTER THIRTY-EIGHT

Ned stopped at a creek to rest his horse and let him drink water. He loosened the saddle girth, then staked his horse where he could eat some grass. He got some food out of his grub bag and his canteen from the saddle horn, settling on some jerky and the rest of the cold, hard, stale biscuits he had bought in Boswell a few days back. When he was through eating, Ned took his horse back to the creek and let him drink some more water while he filled his canteen. He took off again at a fast pace. He would run when he could and walk when he had to.

He knew where he was heading and could find his way even in darkness, so he kept on past sunset, arriving at Salt Creek well after dark. This particular creek ran into the Kiamichi River, and from there it wasn't far to the old military road that would take him to Gilbert.

The ground was turning sandy with scattered

gravel and rocks. He was letting his horse walk at his own pace now.

He came up to the old military road that was used to take supplies between Fort Washita and Fort Towson back in the day. It wasn't used by the military anymore, but he and his horse were familiar with the area and had been on this same road more than once. Brush and saplings were now sprouting in the middle of the road.

When he thought he was close enough to his destination to make camp, Ned stopped for the night and built a small fire. It was going to be a long cold night, but he'd make it just fine. He ate a small supper before making his bed and lying down to sleep.

He was awake before daylight. He was cold and sore from sleeping on the hard ground. He moved stiffly as he saddled his horse. Soon he was on his way again, heading east toward the Kiamichi River.

It was breaking daylight when the old road led him to the river crossing.

The Army had built a rock dam across the river years ago. Below the dam was an old road where supply wagons could travel across the water. Ned guided his horse through the shallow, swift water and up the other bank.

A few hundred yards beyond the river was a road that went south. Eventually it would take him to Gilbert, Indian Territory. As he rode, he considered his plan. Should he go to the livery stable first to see if they would buy his horse and saddle, then do the rest of his business? He really didn't want to stay at the hotel so he decided to ride around the outskirts of town and see if there was a house close to the depot where he could stay until he could catch the train tomorrow.

CHAPTER THIRTY-NINE

Throwing back the covers of his bedroll, Card's muscles and joints were sore and stiff from the hard, cold ground. He was ready to find Ned and kill him so he could get back to a normal life and stop sleeping on the cold, hard ground. After he heated up his coffee and ate some jerky for breakfast, time was wasting and he needed to hit the trail.

He rode at a slow lope until he came to Salt Creek, right before noon. He let Smoke drink and graze while he ate some more of Mrs. Marshall's jerky. He forced himself not to think about Jean. He had to keep his mind focused on catching up with Ned and killing him.

He walked Smoke across the creek and up the opposite bank and could still make out Ned's horse tracks heading to the south. When he came to a little rocky area, the tracks stopped.

He rode in a circle around the perimeter, but didn't

see any tracks, so he rode a bigger course and finally picked up tracks going east.

He followed east, riding at a slow lope and walk. After about an hour later he saw where someone had made camp.

Dismounting, he felt around in the coals and they were still warm. He was still on the right trail and not far behind Ned.

The trail took him to an old road. He saw where the rider was using the lane to continue on east.

It looked like the road hadn't been used in years. Fortunately, the path was still visible, and Card had no trouble tracking his man.

He stayed on the road until he came up to the Kiamichi River. A horse had walked into the water below a rock dam. Now Card pulled his rifle out and laid it across the front of his saddle just in case Ned or one of his hired friends were hiding on the other bank, waiting to shoot him as he crossed the river.

When he was on the other side, he found the tracks again. They turned south onto a road that went through pastures and farmland. Farther down the road he began to see houses along the path. He figured he must be getting close to a town.

CHAPTER FORTY

N ed rode on the eastern outskirts of the town to get a layout of the main streets and railroad tracks. He stayed in the timber as much as possible and made a wide swath around the settlement. He came to Rock Creek and turned back southwest where he found the main east–west road.

On the road not far from the train depot was a small house to the south that was partially hidden from view by trees. He rode on past it until he saw the train station.

That house off the road would do nicely for his stay in town, so he circled back and turned down the path to the residence.

He dismounted and walked up to the house, pulling his folding knife out of his back pocket and hiding it behind his back. He knocked on the door and waited. The door opened and an elderly woman asked, "What do you want?"

"Ma'am, is your husband home?" asked Ned.

"My husband passed two years ago," she said. "Now state your business or leave."

Ned moved swiftly and stuck the knife in her chest. She gasped for air as he twisted it deeper.

Using his other hand, he pushed her back into the house. She was dead in his arms, so he let the knife stay in her chest preventing her blood from getting on everything. He dragged her to another room and laid her on the floor before finally pulling the knife out and wiping the blood off on her dress. Then he put it away.

Ned searched the old woman's body for money. He looked down the front of her dress, and sure enough there was a little bag pinned to the inside of the fabric. He jerked it out, removed $530 from the pouch.

Next, he walked around the house and searched for anything else he might want. He found a roasting pan sitting on the cookstove. In it was a large roast with carrots, taters, and onions. He found a knife and fork and ate some right out of the pan. He smacked his lips and said, "This is really good food, I'm so appreciative you made it for me, ma'am."

When he finished eating, he went to get his gear off his horse and brought all of it into the house and put it in the woman's bedroom.

He unbuckled his gun belt and left it there also. He didn't want anyone to see him wearing his fancy gun. He mounted his horse, heading back the way he'd come.

Ned wanted to enter town from the north since he'd be staying on the south side.

He rode in on the same road that came from the river crossing, and walked his horse to the livery stable and dismounted. Finally, a man came out of the tack room carrying a bucket.

"Howdy stranger, can I help you with something?"

"I want to sell my horse and saddle," said Ned. "I don't need them anymore."

The man walked around the horse and looked him over. When he got to the animal's head, he took hold of the horse's lower jaw and opened his mouth to look at his teeth. Next the livery owner lifted the horse's front foot to examine his hoof. He went to the saddle and picked up a stirrup to examine the leather and looked at the girth strap.

When he finished his thorough examination, he said, "I'll pay you sixty dollars for both the horse and saddle together."

Ned shook his head. "You know dang well they are worth way more than that."

"Not to me," said the man. "I've got to buy them cheap enough so I can make something. I'm in business to make money. You can take it or ride on out of here."

Ned didn't want to cause any trouble, so he acted like he was put off by the offer but finally said, "Okay, I know the horse is worth more than that but I understand you've got to make money. If the offer still stands, I'll take it."

"You wait here, and I'll be right back with the money." The man returned to the tack room and emerged with sixty dollars cash.

He handed the money to Ned. "I hope it's no hard

feelings, but I've got to make something off my purchases."

Ned took the money. "I think it's highway robbery, but I need to get rid of the horse today." He walked away from the livery stable toward the dry goods store.

I should come back here before I leave and kill him for lowballing me on my horse.

He went into the store and picked himself out a new shirt, britches, and vest. He couldn't wait to take a hot bath and see what he looked like in new duds. He carried his stuff up to the counter where he noticed some handguns in a glass case.

"I want one of those new Colt revolvers and two boxes of shells," said Ned.

"Yes, sir. These are the latest models and are selling like hotcakes," said the clerk.

He put the gun on the counter. Ned picked it up and spun the cylinder then looked down the barrel before setting it back down.

"Would you like one of these new leather holsters to go with your gun?" the clerk asked. "It's only eight more dollars."

"No," replied Ned. "Just figure up my bill so I can be on my way."

"How about one of those new Texas-style hats over there on the wall? They're hot sellers right now and only three dollars," said the clerk.

Ned looked at the hats and tried a few on. He found one that fit nicely and set it on the counter with his other things.

The man took a pencil and paper and added up the bill. "That comes to ninety-two dollars."

Ned pulled his roll of money out and paid the man.

"Would you like everything in a bag?" asked the clerk. "I've got some brand-new paper sacks that are so useful."

Ned thought that was a good idea. "Yeah, put everything in the sack except the gun, I'll carry it in the front of my britches."

He left the store and walked to the barbershop. No one was in the chair, so he sat down and told the barber he wanted a shave and haircut.

"Would you like your hair washed for an extra dime?" asked the barber.

"Sure, go ahead," replied Ned.

The barber had a small metal tank over the sink with a hose attached to a valve. He left the room and came back in with two buckets of water that he poured in the tank. He leaned the barber chair back so Ned's head was in the sink. The barber opened a valve on the bottom of the tank and started wetting his hair.

He applied soap and worked it in with his hands. When Ned's hair was covered in suds, the barber rinsed the soap out with the hose. He sat Ned back up and dried his hair with a towel, then picked up a pair of scissors and began cutting.

The barber started asking Ned questions. Ned couldn't tell if the man was trying to make small talk or was just being nosy.

"I'm not in the mood to talk," said Ned. "Just cut my hair and be quiet."

When he was finished with Ned's hair, the barber put some water in the shaving mug and swirled the brush around in it until it was lathered up. He proceeded to put shaving soap all over Ned's face. Then the barber opened his straight razor and picked up the leather strap to hone the blade. Ned reached under the barber sheet that was covering his lap. He pulled his gun out of the front of his britches and laid it in his lap, just in case the barber made a mistake with that straight razor.

Ned sat still as a statue while he was getting shaved. When the barber was finished, he left the room again and came back with a hot towel that he wrapped around Ned's face. Ned eased his gun back into the front of his britches.

The barber removed the towel and said, "I'm finished. Here's a mirror so you can look at the haircut."

Ned stood up, looked at himself in the mirror, and handed the barber a dollar. "Much obliged," he said and picked up his sack of clothes and walked to the house where he was staying.

After a bath he put on new clothes, buckled on his gun belt with the new gun, along with the new hat. The reflection in the mirror was a different man and no one would ever recognize him.

It was time to check on when the next eastbound train would be, he went to the front window and looked around to make sure no one was watching the house. Then walked to the depot, where he went to the ticket window and asked the ticket agent, "When's the next eastbound train?"

"That'll be tomorrow," said the agent. "It leaves the station at ten o'clock sharp."

Ned walked back to the house and put wood in the stove to warm his supper. After the meal, he loaded up the fireplace with wood. No cold, hard ground for him tonight.

CHAPTER FORTY-ONE

After turning south on the road, Card had ridden about a mile when he made his way up a hill where there was a town. Stopped along the side of the road, he removed the thong off his gun, Ned could be waiting on him, but then he remembered that Ned had never tried to shoot him at a town. He wanted to ride through the town and get an idea of what was there. There was a livery stable, a dry goods store, two banks, and a hotel on Main Street. On the next street over, was a couple of churches, a grist mill, a cotton gin, and a train depot. Next to the depot was a crosstie yard, so there was probably a sawmill nearby.

A road going east and west south of the railroad tracks seemed to be the main road in and out of town.

Card rode across the railroad tracks and turned west and rode past the cotton gin. The road dropped down into the river bottom and went all the way to the river, where there was a ferry.

He asked the ferry operator, "Has a man wearing

black clothes and a fancy pearl-handled gun ridden on your ferry today?"

"No, ain't nobody been across wearing black today," said the man.

Card tipped his hat. "Much obliged."

He went east down the road until he came to Rock Creek. Not seeing any tracks that indicated Ned had come that way, he turned Smoke around and rode back into town. To be certain that Ned had come this way, he would have to start asking questions.

The livery stable would be the first stop.

After dismounting, he tied up Smoke to the hitch rail and went into the stable.

"What can I do for you?" asked the stable owner.

"I am looking for a man," Card said. "He's wearing black clothes and carrying a pearl-handled gun."

"Someone in black did come in here earlier today, but he didn't have a gun on at all that I could tell," the stable owner said. "I bought his horse and saddle because he said he didn't need them anymore."

"Did he say why he didn't need them anymore?" asked Card.

"No, he just wanted to sell them."

"Much obliged," said Card. He started to leave, but then turned back around and asked, "Did you happen to see which way the man headed?"

"I reckon he went to the dry goods store over yonder," he said, pointing down the street.

"Thanks," said Card and went down the street watching for Ned, while he tied Smoke to the post outside the store.

The store clerk was behind the counter dusting off the top of some tin cans.

"Howdy, sir," said Card. "Have you had a customer in today wearing black clothes?"

"Yep, he was in here earlier today buying new clothes, a hat, and a gun," said the clerk.

"Can you describe the new clothes and hat that the man purchased?" asked Card, while pulling five dollars out of his pocket and laying it on the counter.

The man took one look at the money and said, "He bought one of these new Texas-style hats." He took one off the wall and set it on the counter. Then the clerk walked to the clothes stacked on a table and picked up a brown shirt and a pair of denim britches. "He purchased a change of these also."

"You said earlier that he bought a gun," said Card.

"Yes sir," said the clerk, then went behind the counter and picked up a gun. "The man wanted one of these new Colt revolvers and two boxes of shells. He stuck the gun in the front of his britches when he walked out."

Tapping his fingers lightly on the countertop. "Do you know where he went or what direction he took when he left here?" asked Card.

The clerk motioned to the south. "I believe he was heading to the barbershop. I put all his stuff in one of these new paper bags." The store clerk held up a brown paper sack.

"Thanks for the information," said Card. "If you happen to see the man again, I'll pay if you'll send someone after me at the hotel."

The clerk walked to the window. "I know he

headed south when he left here. I was curious, so I watched him go in the barbershop."

"Thanks for the information," said Card as he went outside and walked to the barbershop.

The barber was busy cutting someone's hair, so Card sat down and waited until he was finished and the customer left. Card took out five dollars and went to the chair and laid the money down on the seat. "Did you have a customer in here dressed in black clothes today?"

The barber took one look at the five dollars and his loose mouth started talking. "Yes sir, he came in today and I washed his hair over here at the sink. Then I cut his hair and gave him a shave."

"Did he mention where he was going or maybe where he is staying in town?" asked Card.

"Oh, no sir," he said. "He was in no mood to talk and told me to mind my own business when I tried to make conversation."

"Did you notice anything else about him?" Card asked.

"He had a gun in the waist of his britches and I'm pretty sure he laid it in his lap when I started shaving him."

"Anything else you can think of?"

"He gave me a dollar when I was finished and left. All I know is he turned south when he walked out the door."

Card left the money on the chair and went outside, mounted his horse and rode to the hotel.

No one was at the counter, so he rang the bell, and

a woman came out a door and asked, "Do you need lodging for the night, mister?"

"Yes, I do, and maybe some information," said Card. "Did a man wearing black clothes come in here today?"

She pushed the register book and pen toward him. "Mister," she said, "You're the only new customer I've had in two days. That'll be four dollars for the room. If you want a bath, that's another two dollars."

Card handed her some money. "I do want the bath but not until dark, and can I get a room upstairs with a window that overlooks the street?"

She handed him a key and said, "You're upstairs in number twenty-five."

It was modest accommodations with a bed, a nightstand, washbasin, and chair. He put his stuff on the bed and moved the chair to the window.

He sat down, looking out at the street.

Why had Ned sold his horse and saddle?

Why did he buy new clothes and a gun?

Why is he not at the hotel?

All these questions were bothering Card. He couldn't figure out what Ned was up to.

Card could see from the livery stable all the way to the other side of town to the train depot from his window.

So, this was Gilbert, Indian Territory. Why would anyone come here?

Then he laughed. "Ned Black, how dumb do you think I am!"

Card got up and went downstairs and out the door. He mounted Smoke and headed to the depot, where he walked up to the ticket window and asked the station master, "Has a man in black clothes bought a ticket today?"

"No sir," said the agent.

Card stood thinking for a moment. "How about a man with a Texas-style hat and brown shirt, with a fresh shave and haircut? Has anyone like that been here today?"

"Well now, a feller did come by a little bit ago inquiring about when the next eastbound was. I told him ten o'clock tomorrow morning. He left without buying a ticket."

"Thanks for the information," said Card. He got on his horse and headed to the livery stable.

He left Smoke there for the night with instructions that he wanted him fed and rubbed down.

Card went to the café and ordered supper. They had beef steak, sweet taters, beans, and cornbread. When the waitress came over, he asked, "Has a man dressed in a Texas-style hat and brown shirt been in today?"

"No, you're the only stranger that's come in today," she said.

Still no sign of Ned.

The meal was good and hit the spot. He paid for his food and went back to the hotel. He walked up to the counter, where a man was looking at the register book.

"I'm ready to take my bath whenever the water's ready," said Card.

The hotel clerk replied, "Sir, it's ready now in the

room at the end of the hall. There are towels and soap on the table in the washroom."

Card went up to his room and got his travel bag and went back downstairs to the washroom. The bathwater was waiting on him, and he took off his clothes, got in the tub, and washed up. The hot water felt good on his tired body. His shoulder was still a little tender from the fight he'd had a few days ago. Hopefully the hot water would take some of the soreness out.

When he was finished, he put on clean clothes and left his towel and a dollar sitting on the table.

Card went back to the hotel counter and asked, "Do you have laundry service?"

"We'll be glad to wash your clothes tomorrow," said the clerk.

He laid five dollars on the counter. "I need them washed tonight. I'll need to pick them up in the morning." The man nodded his head and called for his wife to come and get the clothes.

Card went back up to his room and put his things away. He sat at the window and watched the street again while he planned out his strategy for the next day. Ideas came together as he went over and over the plan in his mind, until he was satisfied with it. It was time to go to bed and get some sleep.

CHAPTER FORTY-TWO

C ard slept later than usual; he wasn't in a hurry today. Eventually he got dressed and strapped on his gun belt. He pulled his gun from the holster and opened the cylinder to check his bullets, and also checked the two-shot derringer that he then put in his pocket. He made sure once more that everything was in place before walking to the mirror to comb his hair.

He went to the lobby and asked the hotel clerk if they had breakfast, or would he need to go to the café. The clerk informed him that they had an excellent cook and breakfast was in the dining room. He pointed down a hallway toward the back of the hotel.

Card went down the hall to the dining room. It was small but very nice, with white tablecloths and napkins. He sat facing the door. The waitress came to his table carrying a coffee pot and a cup.

She put the cup down and filled it with coffee. "We've got fresh eggs, ham, taters, and biscuits for breakfast."

He took a sip of his coffee. "I'd like six eggs fried, with the yolks runny," said Card.

She smiled and went to the kitchen. When she came back with the food, he ate in silence and savored every bite. The clerk had been right, it was excellent food.

When the woman came back in to take his dirty dishes away, he gave her two dollars and told her the food was delicious. He then asked, "Is there a lawman in town?"

"No," she said. "We have to depend on the US Marshals out of Fort Smith. Judge Parker is the US Federal Judge over Indian Territory for now and he resides over the law here for now."

"Can you tell me where the telegraph office is located?" asked Card.

She shifted the dishes in her arms. "It's on the west end of the depot. You can't miss it if you walk around the platform. Oh, and your clothes will be dry in about two hours or so," she informed Card.

"That's fine," he replied. "I really appreciate you washing them on such short notice."

Card left the hotel and walked to the depot.

He found the telegraph station on the west end of the building. Inside the office he told the operator, "I need a pen and paper so that I can send an urgent message."

The operator handed him the items he requested and said, "It will cost you a penny a word for the telegram."

Card took the pen and paper and composed a message.

JUDGE PARKER: BE ADVISED, I'M CARD JORDAN.

I'VE KILLED THE NED BLACK GANG. NED, SMOKEY, BILL, TC, AND BIG BOB. GANG MEMBERS' BODIES TURNED IN TO LOCAL LAW FOR PROCESSING REWARDS. CARRYING NED TO LAMAR COUNTY, TEXAS TO SHERIFF GOSE.

Card handed the paper to the operator. "Send this to Judge Parker in Fort Smith, Arkansas immediately."

"Yes sir," said the operator.

"Do not say one word about this to anyone, or I'll take you to Judge Parker myself," Card stated. "Is that clear?"

The operator nodded his head. "Yes, sir."

Card paid him and walked outside.

He looked over at the tie yard and there were stacks of crossties on the ground, partially hidden from view by anyone standing at the ticket window.

He walked to the crossties and found a place to sit down where he could look in between the stacks of timbers to observe the ticket window. He was confident no one on the platform could see him.

Now it was time to wait and be patient. Ned would be here in time for his death.

CHAPTER FORTY-THREE

Ned woke up in his comfortable, warm bed. He smiled at his good luck in acquiring first-class accommodations. He threw the covers back, sat on the side of the bed a minute, then got up to get dressed. He put his new clothes back on, combed his hair, and practiced his draw in the mirror. He went into the kitchen and stoked up the fire to warm up what little roast was left over from last night.

He looked around for coffee but couldn't find any, or even a coffee pot. He did find a water kettle and some tea. That would have to do.

When the water was boiling, he removed it from the stove and poured some in a cup. The tea went next, and he waited for the water to turn brown.

He slurped a sip, and it was bitter and he made a bitter face. Searching through the cupboard, he found a sugar bowl and added some to the tea.

He took another sip, and it was delicious this time.

Not wanting to get to the depot too early, he

searched the house again and found a pocket watch; it must've belonged to the woman's dead husband.

An old newspaper from Fort Smith was on a shelf, so he sat down and read it.

When it was almost time to go, he put his travel bag on the kitchen table. Then picked up a kerosene lamp and took it into the room where the old woman was lying in a pool of dried blood. He put it on the floor against the wall and lit the wick. Then he jerked one of the curtains off the window and draped it over the lamp.

Ned walked back to the kitchen, picked up his bag, and casually left for the depot. When he arrived at the main road he looked back at the house. Smoke was beginning to come out the windows.

He smiled at his handiwork and kept walking like he didn't have a care in the world. Ned was heading up to the platform at the depot when he saw people running in the direction of the old woman's house. That fire should keep the whole town busy for a while, he thought.

At the ticket window, he told the clerk he wanted a ticket to Little Rock, Arkansas.

"That'll be sixteen dollars and seventy-five cents," said the ticket agent.

Ned counted out the money, not paying attention to anything else going on around him.

All of a sudden, he heard a voice behind him that sent a cold chill down his spine.

"Well, I'll be doggone! If it ain't the infamous Ned Black, in the flesh."

Ned recognized the voice as the same one from up

at the hideout. Anger reddened his face when he realized that Joe hadn't killed the gunman. Now he would have to face the man himself.

Turning around slowly, he lowered his hand to hover over his gun.

In front of him was a young man, tall with broad shoulders, and wearing a Calvary hat. Ned was scared, and he was beginning to sweat. He had to think of a plan quickly.

"Excuse me, but I think you have me confused with someone else," said Ned.

"No, I know who you are. I never forget someone who's tried three times to have me killed," said Card. "No wait, make that five times. Those first two times you actually had the guts to try it yourself."

Ned took a step forward. "Boy, you're messing with the wrong man. But before I kill you, I would like to know exactly who you are."

Ned was trying to find an advantage; some way he could distract the young gunman just long enough to have an edge.

"I told you the other day. I'm Card Jordan, and you know my family. You and your murdering gang killed them over in Red River County over two months ago. I've already killed your friends, and now it's time for you to pay your dues and die."

Ned smiled as he looked Card in the eyes while trying to build up his courage. He knew he was going to kill this would-be gunslinger today, just like he had killed his family. He dropped his bag from his left hand and at the same time went for his gun with his right hand. He took hold of his gun and pulled it clear of his holster and started to bring it up to fire.

The first shot hit Ned in the stomach. The pain was excruciating as he stumbled backward from the impact. He looked down at the blood covering his shirt. His eyes got big with rage and couldn't believe this kid had shot him after he'd already had his gun in his hand.

He mustered all the strength he had in him to raise his gun.

CHAPTER FORTY-FOUR

Card took a step forward. "This is for my family. Now they can rest in peace."

He shot Ned through the heart and the lifeless body tumbled to the ground of the platform.

Card ejected the spent shells and reloaded his gun. He looked over at the ticket agent. "I have wanted posters on this man."

The ticket agent was white from fear and silently nodded his head in acknowledgment.

"I'm going to the livery stable for my horse and to buy a packhorse for his corpse. Don't let anyone touch the body until I get back. Then I'll load him up and take him to the sheriff in Paris, Texas, so he can process the reward."

The ticket clerk was so frightened, all he could do was keep nodding his head.

Card walked to the livery stable and noticed men running in the opposite direction down the street. He looked in that direction and saw smoke billowing into the sky. He figured a house fire to be the cause of all the commotion and continued to the livery stable.

No one was there, so he decided to walk on to the hotel and collect his things. He entered the hotel, and the same woman from the day before was working the counter. He informed her that he was leaving and needed to check out. She hurried out to the back and returned with a stack of clean, dry, folded clothes.

"We really appreciate you staying with us, and I hope you come back again sometime. You're always welcome here, Mr. Jordan," she said.

Card smiled. "Thanks ma'am, it's been a pleasure."

Then he went up to his room and grabbed his travel bag and walked back to the lobby. "Do you know what happened south of town, where the smoke is?" he asked.

"Mrs. Hamby's house is on fire," she said. "I sure hope she's all right; she's such a nice lady."

"Thanks again." He tipped his hat and went back to the livery stable.

CHAPTER FORTY-FIVE

Card glanced to the south. The smoke had died down considerably, and people were coming back into town. He walked into the corral, caught Smoke and put the bridle on him. The livery owner came back as he was leading Smoke inside the stable. "I'm leaving and need to buy a horse and pack saddle off you, if you have any for sale," said Card.

"The only horse I've got for sale is the one I bought off that feller yesterday," he replied. "I need to get a hundred dollars for him and the packsaddle. He's a good sound horse."

Card reached into his pocket and pulled out some money. He counted out one hundred dollars and handed it to the man. "I want a bill of sale for him just in case someone decides to try and claim him."

"I'll get you one." He went to the tack room and came back with a piece of paper and handed it to Card.

"I'll go get the horse and put that packsaddle on him for you," he mumbled, hurrying off to the corral.

A few minutes later, he came back inside the barn with the horse and put the packsaddle on.

Card walked toward the back of the stable. "I'll be back in a few minutes."

He walked to a large tree and leaned his back against it. This was the first time he had the chance to be alone and rejoice that it was done. He needed to be alone and collect his emotions. The hunt was over. What a relief it was to finally kill Ned. He was suddenly tired and felt drained of energy. He had fulfilled his promise to his family and now it was time to get on with his life.

After he had cleared his mind and come to grips with killing Ned, he walked back into the stable.

"Do you have any rope I can buy?" he asked. "I need to tie a dead body on the packhorse."

The man looked frightened. Card smiled reassuringly. "I shot that man that came in here yesterday wearing black, and I'm taking his body to Sheriff Gose in Paris to claim the reward."

"So, he was an outlaw!" the man said enthusiastically.

Card nodded. "Yes, he was an outlaw that I have been hunting for over two months. He was murdering scum and got what was coming to him. I'm relieved that it's finally over and may he rot in hell."

The stable man coiled up the lead rope in his hand. "If you don't mind, what was his name?"

"Ned Black. He and his gang are all dead. They

murdered my family and that's why I was after him," said Card.

"I've heard of him. You take care," the man said.

Card mounted Smoke and took the lead rope from the man and started to the depot to collect Ned's body.

He could still see a little smoke coming from the burned house south of town.

As he rode to the depot, he heard the train coming into town. It was blowing its whistle in multiple short blasts. A few locals stood close to the tracks waiting on its arrival.

Card tied his horses to a post and removed the tarp and some rope from the back of his saddle. He cut four length of rope and spread them on the ground and then spread the tarp on top of the rope.

Card searched through Ned's pockets and found a watch, a knife, and his money. He put everything in his pockets, then rolled Ned over onto the tarp and folded it tightly around Ned's body and tied it with the rope.

Men were coming back from the fire now and saw Card tying the tarp around Ned.

They came over and asked, "What are you doing, and who's that dead man?"

Card stopped his work and stood up. "My name is Card Jordan, and this dead man is a murdering thief who killed my family. His name is Ned Black. I'm going to load him up and take his corpse to Sheriff Gose in Paris to process the reward."

One man spoke up and said, "Sam Walters said that right before Mrs. Hamby's house caught fire, he saw a man in a brown shirt carrying a bag walking up the path from her house."

Card untied one of the pieces of rope and opened up the tarp. He said, "Take a look and see if this is the man."

"Oh, I didn't see him, but if you'll wait for a few minutes, I'll go fetch Sam, and he can identify him," replied the man.

Card nodded. "Go get Sam and be quick about it."

The train had stopped at the depot, and men were unloading mail sacks and some cargo. Even though it wasn't moving, the train was still extremely loud as it sat there idling and blowing steam out the petcocks.

After about ten minutes, the train pulled away, leaving behind steam and smoke.

Card asked the other men, "What's the fastest way to Paris, Texas, by way of a road?"

They pointed to the west.

"Ride down to the Kiamichi River," said one man. "There's a ferry you can use to cross on. Continue west for about three miles, then you'll see a wagon trail that goes south. Follow that until it turns west. You will eventually intersect with the north–south road going to Paris."

"I'm familiar with the road that goes to Paris," said Card.

The other man and Sam came back. Sam looked at the late Ned Black.

"Yep, that's the man I saw walking up the lane from Mrs. Hamby's house," he affirmed. "We've determined that she was killed before the house was set on fire."

Sam told everyone that the first men there could see her in the side room. She was on the floor with blood everywhere and she looked like she had been dead for a while.

"Ned must have killed her yesterday and used her house to hide until he could get a train out of here today," said Card. "I'll notify Judge Parker over at Fort Smith about Ned's latest victim."

The telegraph operator was standing on the platform, listening. He spoke up and said, "I'll take care of that for you at no charge. Mrs. Hamby was a friend of mine."

"Mister, you need to get started on your way to Paris. That body is liable to start stinking before long," one of the men commented.

A couple of the men helped Card lift Ned onto the horse and secure the body. He mounted Smoke and someone handed him the lead rope. He gave it a tug and they rode toward the road south of the depot.

The road passed by the crosstie yard and the cotton gin. He went down an incline to the river bottom. When he reached the Kiamichi River, the ferry was docked at the platform, so he rode across the platform and right onto the barge where he paid the man a quarter to pull the barge across the river using cables stretched from bank to bank.

Once on the other side, the horses had a steep climb back to the road. The new pack horse was not used to being led and it took a few miles before he finally quit struggling and followed Smoke without difficulty.

Card took the wagon trail that turned south and

followed it until it turned west. Then they slowed to a walk for a few minutes to give the horses a breather.

At the first creek he came to, he let the horses drink their fill, then continued on his way, riding the horses harder now. He maintained this speed until he came to the main road going south to Paris. From what he could remember, it couldn't be more than ten miles to the Red River.

Keeping up the pace, he glanced over at John Henry and Mary's house as he went by. Someone was in the field plowing with two mules and he assumed it was John Henry. Card took his hat off and waved it in the air as he rode by. John Henry saw him and waved back.

When he was about a quarter of a mile from Red River, he slowed the horses to a leisurely walk to give them time to blow. As he came up to the river, he could see on the opposite bank the same folks from the other day, still camped as before.

Once across the river, Card rode up the trail that took him by their camp and got that feeling in his stomach that told him something wasn't right. Reaching down with his hand, he removed the safety strap off his gun. When he rode up to the campsite, there were two strangers sitting at the fire with the other folks.

They were two hard-looking unfamiliar men, heavily armed. Card could tell by the frightened look on the settlers' faces, especially the women and kids, that something was going on. Continuing into the camp, he stopped his horse and looked closely at the settlers.

"Is everything okay here?" he asked.

The two hard cases stood up, making sure to show their guns to Card.

"Boy, it's none of your business what goes on here," one of them said.

"You're absolutely right, sir, it's none of my business what goes on here," said Card.

"Who you got in that tarp?" the other one asked. "We may want to take him off your hands."

"I've got Ned Black, not that it's any of your business."

The man spit tobacco juice on the ground. "Well, we might want to make it our business."

Card moved Smoke to the left one step. "Oh yeah? How are you planning to do that?" he asked, with a hard, stern look on his face.

Both men went for their guns.

Card palmed his gun and fired as fast as he could, move his thumb and trigger finger.

Both men fell backward from the impact of the .44 bullets. Both were dead before they hit the ground.

Card opened the cylinder on his gun and ejected the spent shells and reloaded.

The families were all huddled up together, shaking in fear.

"Folks, it's over with and these men are dead," announced Card. "Do you know who they are?"

"They're Harold and Tom Hays and they're outlaws from across the river in Indian Territory," said one of the settlers. "We were afraid they were going to kill us and take our wagons and women. We're peaceful, God-loving folks, and this here is all we have, mister." He spread his arms toward his wagon.

"You load their bodies in the back of your wagons and take them to Sheriff Gose in Paris," said Card. "I'm sure there's a reward on them. You can also have all their valuables, including their horses and saddles. That should be enough to get you where you are going."

"We can sure use that money, thank you!" said the other man.

"I'll be on my way now," Card said. "I'll let the sheriff know you're bringing them in."

The settlers walked over to where Card was sitting on his horse.

"We can never repay you for what you have done for us today," said the first man. "Would you mind if we pray for you before you leave?"

Card removed his hat and bowed his head as the man prayed. When he was finished Card headed south toward Paris.

CHAPTER FORTY-SIX

P aris was coming into view as the sun was beginning to set. Card had to slow his horses down to a walk as he made his way down the main street.

The sheriff's office was next to the courthouse, right before he got to the square.

He found a hitch rail to tie the horses to and went inside. Sheriff Gose and three deputies were sitting at desks drinking coffee.

The sheriff looked up and smiled. "Mr. Jordan, what do we have the pleasure of doing for you today? Would you like a cup of coffee?"

"I'd love a cup, Sheriff," said Card. One of the deputies poured him a cup and handed it to him. He took a sip; it was good and strong. Just what he needed after his long ride.

"I brought Ned Black's corpse with me this time, Sheriff," said Card. "He's tied across my pack horse outside."

Card lay the money he took off Ned onto the sheriff's desk. "Will you make sure this money gets back to the bank in Reno? I killed him over in Indian Territory this morning. I've already sent Judge Parker a telegram letting him know. Now Ned and his entire gang are dead. I'd appreciate it if you'd process the reward money and have it sent to my bank back home."

Sheriff Gose smiled and said, "Card, everything is already taken care of. Judge Parker contacted me this afternoon concerning Ned Black and his gang. Just for your information, the judge told me that Ned had a price on his head for $15,000, and each member of his gang was $10,000. Judge Parker processed all the reward money for you plus another two thousand each for those brothers you shot. Son, you're a very rich man."

Card sat there and took another drink of coffee. Then he said, "I'd give it all up to have my family back again."

"I know you would," said the sheriff.

"There'll be some folks coming here tonight or in the morning bringing in the bodies of Harold and Tom Hays," said Card. "I'd appreciate it if you would inquire of any rewards that may be available for those men. These folks need some help and they're good people, just a little down on their luck. I killed those two in self-defense, but I want the folks bringing them in to get the reward money."

"I'll take care of that for you," said Sheriff Gose. He turned to his deputies. "Go get Ned off that horse and contact the undertaker," he directed them.

The sheriff looked at Card for a minute, then asked, "Card, what's your plans now?"

Card sat where he was and looked at the sheriff with tears in his eyes.

"I was a heartbroken boy when I left my home to hunt down those men. I've killed more than my share of men in the last two months. In fact, I hope I never have to kill again. I am not the same broken-hearted kid I used to be; now I'm a grown man with a world of experiences that I hope no other man has to endure. I have a beautiful woman waiting on me out west of town and that's where I'm heading when I leave here. I plan on marrying her and enjoying our life together. If it's all right with you, I'd like to head on over there to see her."

Sheriff Gose stood up and extended his hand. "Card, it's been my pleasure. You go ahead and get on the road. If you want, I can have one of the deputies take your pack horse to the livery stable where your other horses are."

"That would be nice," Card told the sheriff. "Tell the livery stable fellow I'll be back for all my horses in a few days."

CHAPTER FORTY-SEVEN

Card pushed his horse the entire five miles to the Marshall farm. It was dark when he rode into the yard, but lights were on inside the house. He wanted to surprise Jean, so he went to the barn first.

There was a lantern hung on a hook by the door. After retrieving it he found a box of matches and lit it. By the dim light he unsaddled Smoke and turned him into the corral. Next, he removed his chaps and hung them on a peg, then picked up his grub and travel bags and walked to the house.

The walk to the front door seemed to take ages. He eased up onto the porch, opened the door quietly and walked into the house.

He could hear talking coming from the kitchen, so he tiptoed to the doorway and said, "Is there room for one more at the table?"

Jean jumped up from her chair and ran to him. She hugged and kissed him and burst out sobbing from happiness. Then she got serious. "Cord Jordan, you know better than to sneak in here like that, you almost gave me a heart attack," she scolded, hitting his arm lightly.

They both laughed, and Card gave her another hug.

Sue put another plate on the table. "Jean, leave the boy alone and let him eat, I'm sure he's starving."

"Yes, Grandma," said Jean smiling.

Card went to the wash pan, washed his hands, and sat down to eat with the family.

When they were finished, he asked, "Sue, if it wouldn't be too much trouble, I'd like to take a bath. I could sure use one, and some clean clothes."

"I'll put a couple of buckets of water on the stove to heat while me and Jean clean up the kitchen," said Sue.

Jean brought in the washtub from outside while Card went to the well and drew two buckets of water, brought them into the house, and poured them in the tub. He went back out for two more, pouring one in the tub and setting the other one on the stove to heat along with what Sue was already heating up.

When the water was hot, he poured it into the tub.

Everyone stepped out so he would have his privacy. He stripped off and got in the little tub, hardly fitting. But it was a hot bath, and that was all that mattered.

When he finished, he dressed in clean clothes, took the tub back outside, poured out the water, and hung it on the wall. He came into the living room and sat down to join Jean and her grandparents. They all wanted to know how he was and if he was finished with what he had to do.

Card told them about his journey into the Kiamichi Mountains and how Ned had tried to elude him. He explained how Ned escaped from his mountain hide-out, and how he tracked him to a little town on the Kiamichi River named Gilbert.

He spoke about the incident at the Red River while taking Ned to Sheriff Gose in Paris. He didn't go into any details about the two men he killed at the river except that they were bad men and he had killed them in a fair fight.

Jean spoke up first and said, "Card, we know what you did was hard. I prayed for you every day you were on your terrible journey. I hope now that it's over you'll put your gun away and start planning for our future."

He stood up and walked into the kitchen and picked up a dipper full of water, drinking it down. He walked back into the living room.

Jean had a worried look on her face.

He sat down beside her and took her hands in his. "Jean," he said. "There're bad men out there that are murderers, rapists, and thieves. I'll never let people like that hurt my family again. I'll protect my family at all costs. I'm fast with my gun and I hit what I shoot at. Please don't ever ask me to put it away."

She cried and hugged him. "I was wrong to say that to you. I'm so sorry, and I'll never do it again. You're my knight in shining armor, and I love you, Card Jordan."

He smiled. "I'd like to stay with you a few days

before I head out. It'll be nice to spend some time here with you all and rest up."

"We'd love that, son," said Jacob.

That night they spent more time talking until Jacob told them he was tired and ready to turn in. Everyone said their good nights and went to bed.

Card woke up rested. He took his time getting out of bed and putting his clothes on, then came to the kitchen where everyone was already eating and drinking coffee. He sat down and Jean got him a cup of coffee.

"Did you finally decide to get up, sleepyhead?" she teased. "You do realize the day is almost half over."

He smiled and ate his breakfast.

"Jacob, I need some things from town, if you could go later," said Sue.

"I'll go to town for you," said Card. "That way Jacob doesn't have to get out in the cold. In fact, I'm hoping Jean will go with me." He gave her a questioning look and saw the surprised expression on her face. He knew she loved going into town and looking at all the nice new things in the stores.

"Well, I guess that would be fine," said Sue.

"You go get ready while I hitch up the wagon," Card told Jean.

It was cold outside, and he walked quickly to the barn. The water trough was frozen over. He took an axe and broke the ice, and the horses drank thirstily.

The wagon was ready for travel when Jean came out wearing a cape and carrying two quilts. She climbed up onto the wagon and spread one quilt on the seat, sat down and waited for Card so she could cover their legs with the other quilt.

It was about a two-hour ride to town in the wagon. They talked and laughed about nothing in particular the whole way there.

When they got to the mercantile, Card pulled the wagon up to the front and tied the horses off to the hitch rail and helped Jean down.

"Do you have a list of things that Sue needs?" asked Card.

"Yes, I do. Here it is," she replied and pulled a piece of paper from her pocket.

They went into the store and Jean gave the list to the store clerk. She began to browse, looking at clothes and shoes. Card quietly asked the clerk, "Is there someplace in town where I can buy a ring?"

"There's a store called Expressions. It's down the street a way," the clerk said, pointing down the street the way they had come.

Card joined Jean and they looked around at all the things in the store for a few minutes.

Then he took her by the hand and said, "Come on, let's go window shopping."

They moseyed along the sidewalk, looking in windows and having fun and laughing. When they came to Expressions, Card said, "Let's go in here."

They walked into the shop. It sold decorative dishes, fancy dresses, expensive jewelry, and personal items for women. Card took hold of Jean's hand and walked up to the counter.

"We'd like to look at wedding rings, please," he told the woman behind the counter.

Jean almost fainted on the spot.

The look on her face was priceless, Card thought. She was smiling with a glow to her cheeks and a sparkle in her eyes as she held her hands cupped over her mouth, breathing deep breaths.

The lady smiled and went to a large upright safe. She pulled out a display tray and set it on the counter.

Card looked at Jean and said, "Today is your day. Pick out the one you like."

Jean was so excited that her hands were shaking.

"These rings are so expensive! Are you sure about this?" she asked as she looked them over.

He nodded and smiled. "Pick out the one you want and try it on," said Card.

Jean pointed to one that had caught her eye. The lady picked it up and handed it to Jean. She tried it on, but it was a little tight. The lady took it and used a ring-sizing tool to enlarge the band until it was a perfect fit.

Jean was so happy that tears rolled down her cheeks.

"Now go pick out the nicest dress you want, because you should have a dress as beautiful as you are," Card said to her.

Jean walked to a rack of dresses and looked at each one until she found one she adored.

"Card, can I get some shoes to match the dress?"

Card smiled. "Of course. You get whatever you want to go with the dress."

When Jean was finished shopping, Card pulled out his money. "How much do we owe you for all this?" he asked the saleswoman.

"The total bill comes to $117," she said.

CHAPTER FORTY-EIGHT

Card and Jean left Expressions and walked to the café. As they passed by the saloon, two cowhands came out the door and almost collided with them.

The cowboys appeared to have been drinking for a while already that morning. One of them said, "You'll need to watch where you're going."

"I'm so sorry, and I apologize to you men," said Card.

"Hey big fellow, how about I teach you a lesson and take that pretty little lady with me?"

Card stopped, turned around, and moved Jean behind him, out of harm's way.

"Mister, you're about to make a fatal mistake," said Card.

The two men looked at each other as if dumbfounded when someone in the street said, "Hey you two, stop it right now!"

They all turned to see Marshal Thomas standing in the street with his gun in his hand.

"Howdy Card, how're you doing?" he asked.

"I'm doing just fine, Marshal," said Card. "I finished that other matter, and this is my fiancée. We're heading to the café for dinner, if you'd like to join us."

"No thanks, son. I'll let you all eat in peace today," replied Marshal Thomas. "I have a little business to take care of here with these two."

He walked up closer to the two cowboys standing there.

As Card and Jean continued walking, they could hear the marshal talking to the men.

"It's your lucky day," he said to them. "That man would have killed you both. You don't ever want to provoke him into a gunfight. Now get out of here and go home."

Card and Jean had a delicious dinner at the café. When they finished, Jean said, "Card, we can't eat like this every day. We'll both get big as barrels."

They walked around town a little more to work off some of their dinner.

"Jean, it's time we go pick up some stuff at the dry goods store," said Card.

"Card Jordan, are you going to buy the town today?" asked Jean, laughing.

He just smiled and kept walking.

They went into the dry goods store and Card said to the owner, "I need some britches, shirts, socks, drawers, and long johns. I also want another pair of boots."

"Yes, sir," said the owner.

Next Card turned to Jean. "You go look for a good heavy coat and anything else you want."

They both picked out new clothes and boots. Jean wanted some jeans also; she'd never owned a pair of britches, so Card told her to get as many as she wanted.

He paid for all their new clothes and the clerk wrapped everything in brown paper and tied it with string. They left the store, each with both their arms full of new clothes.

They went to the wagon and put all their purchases in the back, then went to the mercantile to get Sue's supplies.

The clerk at the mercantile looked at Jean's hand. "Young lady, did you get that ring today?"

She looked at Card then back at the gentleman and said, "Yes sir, I surely did," and held up her hand and smiled.

He congratulated them both and helped carry their things to the wagon.

Jean opened the package with her new coat in it and put it on. They climbed onto the wagon, and she covered their legs with the quilt before they headed home.

Card stopped the wagon close to the front door of the house, and Jean jumped to the ground and ran to the door. Sue and Jacob came out as Jean began to reach for the handle.

"Look what I have!" Jean shouted. She stuck her hand out so they could see her new engagement ring.

Sue made a fuss and told her how pretty it was. "Honey, it's so big! And it looks wonderful on you."

Jean hugged her and cried, "Grandma, I am so happy. I really love him."

Card and Jacob unloaded the supplies and took them into the kitchen.

Sue looked at all the bundles and said, "I swear, you two bought out the town. What in tarnation is all this stuff?"

They opened their packages, and Jean showed Sue her new dress and shoes.

Card and Jacob began to leave the kitchen when Jean stopped them.

"You two just wait right there," she said. "Grandpa, I've got something for you."

She opened a sack that contained a new shirt and a pair of bib overalls. She handed them to Jacob.

"Thank you so much, I'm going to put these on right now," he said, holding up the overalls proudly.

Next, Jean handed Sue a gift and said, "Grandma, this one is for you. We both love you so much."

Sue opened the package, and in it was a brand-new dress and fancy boots. Sue started crying and hugged Jean and Card.

"This is the nicest thing anyone has ever done for me," she said.

"Go put them on so we can see how they look on you," Card told her.

Sue took off running to her bedroom.

Jean and Card had unpacked all their things. When Sue and Jacob came back into the kitchen, they posed in their new clothes like two kids. After much laughter and showing off, Sue told Jacob, "We'd better go change. We surely don't want to get our new duds dirty doing chores."

Card went outside and led the horses back to the barn. He parked the wagon in its spot and unhitched the team of horses. He turned them into the corral, forked hay in the feed trough, then walked back outside and sat down. He had a lot to think about.

Jean looked out the window and saw him sitting on a bucket with his back to the barn.

"Grandpa, what is Card doing out there, just setting on that bucket?"

"Sometimes a man needs to think and ponder on things," Jacob said. "You'll learn over time to respect his alone time and you might be surprised at the plans and decisions that come out of those thinking sessions. One thing I've learned about this young man is that he's a born leader. He makes plans, he's smart, and has lots of common sense. I believe anyone that knows him will tell you he is one to ride the river with. What I mean is, he has sand in his blood, and he won't back down from trouble and can be counted on in any situation. Now, you go along and help your grandma with supper and leave him be, he'll come in directly."

It was getting dusty dark when Card came back into the house. He went to the wash bucket and washed and dried his hands before sitting down at the table. He sat in silence while Jean set the table. She kept glancing at him while she worked.

CHAPTER FORTY-NINE

When everyone was seated, Jacob said a prayer. Then Sue passed around bowls of food. Card was eating in silence when Jacob finally spoke up. "Card, I was thinking. If you ride north a little way to that creek bottom, you might see some turkeys. It'd be nice to have a turkey for dinner."

Card nodded and chewed his food thoughtfully. When he swallowed, he said, "I'll ride over there before daylight tomorrow and see if I can shoot one coming off their roost."

When supper was over, Card asked Sue, "Will you make a pot of coffee? I've got something to discuss with everyone tonight."

When the kitchen was cleaned up, Jean brought cups of coffee into the living room. They sat sipping on it, waiting for Card to speak.

"I've got a plan and would like to go over it with y'all," he said finally.

Jean, Sue, and Jacob watched him expectantly.

"I'll stay here until the day after tomorrow," he continued. "But then I've got to go back home. I've got four horses at the livery stable in Paris, and I need to take them back to my ranch."

He looked at Jacob. "I'd like for you and Sue to sell this farm and all your livestock and anything you don't need. I'll build me and Jean a new house, and you and Sue can live in my family home. I want you close to us; we both need to have family around us."

"How long will you be gone?" asked Jean.

He sat there thinking and said, "I'm going to buy more land and cattle when I get home and I'll need to hire some cowboys to help with the work. I'm not sure how long it'll take, but it shouldn't be more than a few days to a week, I suspect. Jacob, why don't you and Sue take a little time to think about my offer, then we'll discuss it more after supper tomorrow night."

Jacob nodded.

"When I get home," Card said, "I'll have to go to my neighbor's ranch since he is watching after my cattle and house, and tell them my plans. I also have to ride to Maple Springs or Clarksville to hire carpenters to build our house. After I get everything started, I could send a couple of wagons here to haul all your stuff to the ranch. You could bring any household items you want.

"Jean, I know this is probably a surprise to you, but I want to have a big house for lots of kids in the future. I'll provide for you and your family with anything y'all need."

"You're going to a lot of trouble over us," said Jean. "And yes, I want lots of children too."

"Why do you need more land and cattle?" asked Sue. "I thought you already had a ranch."

"I do," said Card. "But I want to pursue a new business venture and I want to leverage my cattle along with it."

"What do you mean, a new business venture?" asked Jean.

"Right now, all the ranches in the area have to make cattle drives into Kansas to sell their herd. I hear that in a few years we'll be able to drive them to Fort Worth," said Card. "That'll be a lot quicker and closer. I plan on buying land and building cattle pens somewhere north of my ranch, so ranchers can load their cattle right onto the train and ship them to the eastern markets. Of course, they'll have to pay to use my pens and loading ramps. But that's in the future. Anyway, I'd appreciate it if you'll take time to think over my plan. We'll discuss your decision tomorrow night."

Card got up at four in the morning and rode to the creek bottom Jacob had told him about, hoping to find a few turkeys. After waiting patiently for an hour or two, he shot two tom turkeys and brought them back home. When he arrived, Jacob helped him pick the feathers off the birds and carry them into the house so Sue could cook them.

Then Card spent the day helping Jacob take the wheels off the wagon and grease them. They worked on repairing harnesses and bridle reins and inspecting the wagon for any loose boards. Card wanted to make sure the wagon was in good shape for the trip to his ranch.

Sue and Jean prepared a large meal with the turkeys that night and after supper, Card and Jacob nodded off in the living room until Jean and Sue came in and sat down.

Sue spoke up first. "I want to discuss us moving to the ranch. I want to know how big the house is. How close will we be to Jean, and how will Jacob make us a living?"

"The house has three bedrooms, a kitchen, a living room, a laundry room, and a water well close by," explained Card. "It is fully furnished but you can bring anything you want from here. Jacob can work for the ranch and his job will be to watch after you, Jean, me, our children, and anything else he sees fit to do. What money you get out of this place is yours. I'll take care of all your expenses for your trip including meals, lodging, and such. All you have to do is ride there."

After some discussion they all agreed this was what they would do.

"In the morning, I'll head to Paris for my horses and then to the ranch and start making arrangements," Card stated.

They stayed up a little later than usual discussing the move. When everyone was ready for bed, Jean said to Card, "You can't imagine how proud I am of you for moving my grandparents close to us. I love you so much, and I know we're going to have a wonderful life together."

He got up early that Friday morning, dressed in

warm clothes, and went into the kitchen. He was surprised to see Jean cooking breakfast. He wrapped his arms around her and kissed the back of her neck.

She said through tears, "I'm going to miss you so much, but I understand you've got things to do for us. I wish I was going with you, although I can wait until you get back. I want you to know, without a doubt, I believe in you, and I love you very much."

Card kissed her, then took a cup and filled it with coffee.

He sat down and had a drink of the scalding coffee then said, "We're going to have a beautiful home, beautiful kids, and a very prosperous life together. Be patient, and just love me."

After breakfast, he packed his travel bag, went out to the barn, and saddled up Smoke.

Jacob had a halter and lead rope on the packhorse that Card had left there after he was shot.

Sue came out and said goodbye. She told Jacob, "You come in the house and let Jean and Card have some time alone."

Jean went to the barn with Card. They hugged and kissed. Card wiped the tears off her cheeks. He looked her in the eyes and said, "I love you. This is not good-bye. It's I'll see you in a few days."

She smiled as he mounted up and headed toward the road. Card stopped one last time and turned back to see Jean waving at him. He put his hand to his mouth and blew her a kiss and urged Smoke to take off.

His first stop was at the livery stable in Paris to

pick up his horses. But before leaving town he decided to get something to drink.

"Feed and water all my horses while I go to the café for coffee?" he asked the stable owner.

"I surely will, Mr. Jordan."

"Mister, just call me Card," said Card as he handed the man the reins.

After two cups of coffee, he went back to the stable and the man had all his horses ready to go, so he paid his bill and mounted up. The horses didn't like being led at first but after a couple of miles, they started trailing along.

To save time, he rode across the countryside as the crow flies, so he could make it home by dark.

He decided to stop at the Lazy H Ranch before going to his own house. He wanted to let Homer Wallace know he was back and give them an update about Ned Black and his gang.

Card saw Homer watching him through the window as he rode up. Homer walked outside to greet him, then rang the dinner bell so everyone would come to the house.

James and Ricky came hurrying up and took the horses and tied them up. Homer had Card come inside and Helen met them as they came through the front door. She told Card, "Come into the kitchen, and I'll fix you a plate of leftovers from dinner." He sat down and ate while the Wallaces waited for him to talk about his journey.

He told them what had happened, where he had been, and about killing each member of the gang. They wanted to ask more questions, but Homer cut them off.

"Card, I need to tell you something. Johnny went over to your place yesterday. He saw horses in the corral and it looked like some men were living in the house. He didn't let them see him, but he watched them for a while. He seems to think they are Mexican bandits that may be traveling through and stealing cattle. He saw a small herd of about sixty cows close by. He came back here to tell me, so I sent him over to Clarksville to the county sheriff to let him know. He should be back any time to let us know what the sheriff is going to do about it."

"I'll wait a little while to see if they come back before I ride to the ranch," said Card.

Meanwhile, he told Homer and the boys how he'd met a girl west of Paris and that he was going to marry her after he took care of some business.

"Card, what's her name?" asked Helen.

"Her name is Jean Marshall," he said.

Helen came over and gave Card a hug. "I am so proud of you, and I want to meet your future wife. I believe we need to plan a big wedding."

"Now hold on, Helen," said Homer. "Card and his bride may already have wedding plans."

"Actually, we don't yet, but I'm sure Jean would love a big to-do ceremony," said Card. "The two of you can talk about it when she gets here."

"Okay, I'll wait and talk to Jean," said Helen, laughing.

"I want to hire someone to build us a house close to my place and build something for some ranch hands to live in. I plan on buying more land and cattle. I was wondering if you might know of some land for sale?"

"Yep, the B Bar Ranch that joins your land to the east is for sale," replied Homer. "Old man Byrd is wanting to move back east to be close to his children. You may be able to buy his place and his cattle. I believe he has six sections of land and probably fifteen hundred head of cattle."

CHAPTER FIFTY

Johnny and Sheriff Taylor rode into the yard around two-thirty. They dismounted and came into the house where everyone was setting in the kitchen talking. Card stood up and shook hands with the sheriff and hugged Johnny.

Sheriff Taylor said, "I'm glad you're here. You've made quite a reputation for yourself, tracking down those killers. I'm hoping you'll ride with me to your ranch house, just in case those fellows over there decide to put up a fight."

"Go saddle the horses and get your guns," Homer told the boys.

"Homer, me and the sheriff will be enough this time," said Card. "Those men won't give the two of us any problems at all."

Card and Sheriff Taylor left the Lazy H together. They knew there could be trouble, but they were ready.

They stopped a good way off to survey the house

and yard. A small herd of cattle grazed on the back side of the creek, but there was no sign of any people.

"Let's ease around and go have a look at those cows," said Card. "I'd like to check the brands on them before we jump to conclusions."

They stayed out of sight from the house and rode to the edge of the herd. From his vantage point, Card could identify four different brands.

Sheriff Taylor saw different brands also. He pointed to a few cows that displayed the Lazy H brand. "That herd is stolen cattle. How do you want to handle this?" he asked Card.

"Let's ride back around and come in behind the barn so it can shield us from their view," Card suggested. "When we get there, I'll dismount and walk as near as I can to the side of the house. Once I'm in position, you ride up and let them know you're here. They'll think you're alone and come out to confront you. Then I'll make my presence known, and it'll be up to them if they live or die."

"Okay, I'm ready," said Sheriff Taylor.

Card tied up Smoke in a low spot behind the barn and snuck around to the side of the house. When he was in position, he waved his hat.

Sheriff Taylor rode into the yard, carrying his Winchester in his arms. He called out, "You men in the house! Come out with your hands up."

Two Mexicans and one White man came out the front door. They spread out and the White man said, "Well hello, Sheriff, why do we have the pleasure of your company today? You're a little outnumbered, hombre."

"You're trespassing on private property and that herd of cattle looks to be stolen. You're under arrest."

They all laughed. The White man yelled, "Sheriff, you're not going to arrest anyone here today."

Card stepped out and said, "Excuse me, but you heard the sheriff. Now drop your gun belts or die right there."

When they looked at Card, the sheriff brought his rifle up and pointed it at the Mexican on the left.

All three bandits went for their guns. Card palmed his Colt and was firing before they ever got off one single shot.

Sheriff Taylor killed the one he had his gun pointed at, and all three cow thieves lay dead in the Jordans' yard.

"Sheriff, are you okay?" asked Card while reloading his gun.

"Yep, I'm just fine."

The sheriff dismounted and checked each man to make sure they were dead. He went through all their pockets and came up with about $5,000, which he handed to Card.

"I ain't never seen no one draw and shoot as fast as you did today," he said to Card. "Son, you are hell on wheels with that six-shooter and can stand with me anytime."

Card only nodded before walking into his house. It was in good shape; they hadn't torn it up much. He came back outside and asked Sheriff Taylor, "What do you want to do with the bodies?"

"We'll load them on their horses, and I'll take them back to town and check wanted posters. I'll put the word out about those brands on the cattle and the owners can come and claim them. If there is any reward money on these fellows, I'll process the paperwork and have the money sent to your bank."

"Thanks, Sheriff," said Card.

Card helped tie the three corpses on their horses, and Sheriff Taylor headed back to Clarksville.

Card put Smoke up for the night and went inside to clean up the mess the cow thieves had made.

The next morning Card started off southeast across the pasture, toward the B Bar, which was less than an hour's ride.

The ranch had been in operation for a long time, and over the years Mr. Byrd had let it get run down. The barn leaned and the house was in need of major repairs. Card stopped at the main house, where he knocked on the door, calling out to Mr. Byrd.

Mrs. Byrd hollered from inside, "Go around to the back. This door won't open no more."

Mr. Byrd was waiting when he came around the corner of the house. "Hello, Mr. Byrd," said Card. "I'm Card Jordan. I live west of you."

"Come on in and have a cup of coffee," said Mr. Byrd.

"We were so sad when we heard about your family," said Mrs. Byrd. "We've been neighbors a long time; your parents were such nice folks."

"Thank you so much, Mrs. Byrd," said Card. "Homer Wallace told me you're thinking about selling the ranch and going back east."

The Byrds nodded in agreement.

"I'd be willing to buy your whole operation—land,

cattle, and any other livestock you have," said Card. "I've got cash money and can finalize the deal anytime you want. If the price is right, that is."

Mr. Byrd sat for a few seconds, looking at his wife before speaking. "We've got six deeded sections of land, and I'm guessing fifteen hundred head of cows and twenty horses. We're thinking a fair price would be twenty-five dollars per acre, and ten dollars a head for cows, and we'll throw in the horses and any other animals roaming the property."

Card thought it over quickly. "I think that's more than a fair price." He reached across the table and shook hands with both of them. "When would you like to sign the papers and get your money?"

"We can do it tomorrow. Meet us in Clarksville at the Red River National Bank at three in the afternoon," said Mr. Byrd.

"That'll be fine. That's where my money is too, so it'll be convenient for us all," said Card.

"Do you have any cowhands that may want to stay on and work?"

"We have two that work full time," Mr. Byrd said. "They might be interested."

"Please tell them they still have a job if they want it," he said. "I'll stop by in a few days to talk to them."

They all shook hands again and Card headed to Clarksville.

CHAPTER FIFTY-ONE

C ard arrived at Clarksville at two in the afternoon and went directly to the bank. The writing on the window said a man named Lloyd Edwards was president of the establishment.

Card went in and introduced himself to the teller. "I'm here to talk to Mr. Edwards," he said.

The teller walked to an office, knocked on the door, and told the man inside he had a client. Mr. Edwards came out of his office and stuck out his hand toward Card.

"I'm Lloyd Edwards. Glad to meet one of our best depositors. What can I do for you, Mr. Jordan?"

"I'd like to talk to you in private," said Card.

They went into the office and took seats.

"I'm buying the B Bar Ranch. Me and the Byrds will be meeting here at the bank tomorrow afternoon at three to sign the papers and make payment. The total amount will be $27,480. I should have that money in the bank but I'm not sure exactly how much I have."

Mr. Edwards picked up a ledger and opened it up. "Card, after the unfortunate death of your family, Sheriff Taylor notified Judge Carter about what happened. The judge had all your family possessions put in your name. With the money that was already in the account plus what you've deposited, you have $86,523.36. You're quite a wealthy man."

Card sat in silence, processing what he had heard.

"Card, if you want to, you can go ahead and sign all the documents concerning the purchase to the B Bar today, since the bank has all the information about the ranch," said Mr. Edwards. "Tomorrow when the Byrds come in you don't even have to show up. I'll handle the transaction for you."

"That'd be great, Mr. Edwards, and just so you know I'm going to build a new house too. But I'll discuss that with you another time."

Card signed all the paperwork for the purchase of the B Bar and left the bank, heading toward home.

He rode through a herd of his cattle grazing in the pasture and noticed two men riding toward him. He took the safety strap off his gun and waited for them to come to him.

"Are you Card Jordan?" one of them asked as they approached.

"Yes, I am, who are you?"

"We ride for the B Bar. I'm Red Snead and this is Jake Toliver," said Red. "Mr. Byrd told us about you buying the ranch."

"It's good to meet you men," said Card. "Are you going to stay on and work for me?"

"Yes sir, we both want to stay on," said Red.

"I pay forty a month plus keep, if that's all right," said Card. "If you know of anyone that wants to work, I'll hire three more hands at the same wages. I'd like a good tally of how many head of cattle we have when you get time. I want to know how many cows, bulls, heifers, and steers are on the B Bar."

"We'll get right on that tomorrow," said Red, "It may take a few days."

"Go ahead and move your things into the big house when the Byrds leave," said Card. "That old bunkhouse is in need of major repairs. I'll be leaving in a few days to move my future wife here, so I'll need for the two of you to watch both this place and mine. If you need anything, just try to take care of it yourselves until I get back."

Card started off toward his house and the two men headed toward the B Bar.

CHAPTER FIFTY-TWO

I t was dark when he arrived back at his home. He fed Smoke and went into the house to cook some supper.

After Card ate, he went out back by the water well with a towel and bar of soap. He stripped off and drew a bucket of water and poured it over his head. It was cold, but he wanted to wash off, so he didn't mind too much. He quickly used the soap and drew another bucket of water to rinse off the suds. Then he picked up his clothes and went back into the house to get ready for bed. Tomorrow would be a long day.

Card stayed in bed until well after daylight the next morning. There were some chores around the house, one of which was to clean up any remaining blood stains left on the floor. But first he wanted to go visit his family so after breakfast he went out back and stood under the tree providing shade for the grave. He kneeled in front of the grave markers and took off his hat.

"I want you to know that I miss you so much. I met a girl by the name of Jean Marshall that I'm going to marry. I'm going after her in a few days and move her and her grandparents here to be with us. I bought the B Bar Ranch and all its cattle yesterday. I want to have a new house built for me and Jean to raise our family in. The new house will be over there," he pointed to his right.

Through tears in his eyes, he said, "Mama, I did what you told me to do. I tracked the murderers down and killed every one of them. I know you watched over me and kept me safe, and I'm so grateful. I love you all so much. I hope those men burn in hell for what they did to us. My prayer is, all of you can rest in peace." Card stood up, hat still in hand. "Pa, by the way, this hat brought me a lot of knowledge and protection. It took two bullets. I'm going to hang it back on the peg in the kitchen and buy me a new hat."

Just then, he heard a horse approaching, and by the sound of the hooves hitting the ground, he figured they were in a big hurry. He stood watching as a lone rider came into view and headed straight toward him.

The rider jerked on the reins and the horse skidded to a stop.

"Are you Card Jordan?" he asked.

"Yeah, I am," Card replied.

"I have an urgent telegram for you." He handed the folded paper to Card, and Card opened it up and read it:

CARD, COME QUICK. URGENT.
JACOB MARSHAL

A LOOK AT BOOK TWO
CARD, MAN OF JUSTICE

From the ashes of vengeance to the heights of danger.

Card Jordan is finally home and eager to start a new chapter with his beloved fiancée after a grueling quest for vengeance. But just as he begins to savor the peace he's fought so hard to achieve, an urgent call pulls him back into the fray. Summoned by a special commission from the president, Card is thrust into a high-stakes rescue mission involving a daring kidnapping scheme.

Before he can even catch his breath, Card receives devastating news from home—news that propels him into a relentless cross-country chase. His mission? To save a young girl from ruthless blackmailers who are tangled in a far-reaching conspiracy that threatens more lives than Card could ever have anticipated.

In a race against time, Card must face off against deadly foes and balance his quest for justice with the personal cost of his mission. Can he unravel the sinister plot, protect those he loves, and restore justice—all while fighting to stay alive?

AVAILABLE NOVEMBER 2024

ACKNOWLEDGMENTS

Writing a book is harder than I thought, and more rewarding than I ever could have imagined. It takes a lot of time, commitment, and inspiration. None of it would have been possible without the support and encouragement from the following people:

Carolyn Garner
Stacy Jones
Tad Garner
Judie Brunson
Ray Sikes
Steve Smith
Sabrina Fox
Ray Gullitt

And a very special thanks to everyone who reads this book.

ABOUT THE AUTHOR

Monty was born and raised in Southeastern Oklahoma in the small town of Sawyer, which is nested along the banks of the Kiamichi River. He's owned horses and cattle, riding the former and working the latter. Over the years, he formed a deep connection and respect for the Old West and the courageous folks who braved the wild frontier.

Monty is an avid reader and is particularly enthusiastic when it comes to Western authors and novels. His love of reading sparked his desire to write his first short story. He loves writing about real places and landmarks from the 1800s. In college, he wrote a ten-page paper about his grandmother, born in 1886, who married at fourteen and took in five orphaned nieces and nephews shortly thereafter. Monty's love for history and penchant for storytelling earned him an A+, and he hasn't looked back since.

Now retired, he loves to travel, fish, spend time with his four grandkids, and tell stories. He looks for inspiration for future books wherever he goes, and he is a member of the Western Writers of America Inc.

www.montygarnerauthor.com

Made in the USA
Monee, IL
07 December 2024

72793701R00184